The Powder Barrel

42
—
62

The Powder Barrel

WILLIAM HAGGARD

IVES WASHBURN, INC.

NEW YORK

IVES WASHBURN, INC., *Publishers*

750 Third Avenue, New York, N. Y. 10017

THE POWDER BARREL

COPYRIGHT © 1965 BY WILLIAM HAGGARD

FIRST AMERICAN EDITION 1965

LIBRARY OF CONGRESS CATALOG CARD NUMBER: 65-23221

MANUFACTURED IN THE UNITED STATES OF AMERICA

For
JULIA BATT

Chapter One

His Highness Shaikh Ali bin Hasan bin Ibrahim could boast a genealogy as extensive as in fact it was mythological, though in practice he never boasted since he was above all things a realist. His great-grandfather had come down to the Coast from the north, and there were rumours that he hadn't been an Arab at all—a Khurd perhaps or even a Turk. But whatever his race he had certainly been successful. His absurd little kingdom was superlatively placed for the matter which had interested him, and that matter had been piracy. It was in fact piracy which had first brought the British to the Coast; they had had an empire to the east of it and its subjects had been complaining. Trade mustn't be interfered with, and it had been a tidy-minded age.

But not the arrangement which had been made with the shaikh. He was independent but he wasn't; he could levy taxation but he couldn't make war; he could maim or imprison his own people but British subjects within the shaikhdom were subject to British law. It had been an international lawyer's nightmare even before the oil had come. Not that Shaikh Ali owned the oil itself: what he owned was a kingdom a hundred miles long by twenty deep, and that hundred miles of coastline held the only usable harbour.

I

The oil came down to it through a complex of pipelines, down to what was by now the third Terminal in the world. His Highness drew his dues on it, His Highness was a ten-percenter.

He was talking now to a man called Stavridis. Stavridis was a Greek, and he had a splendid and much-hyphenated Arab court title. He was in fact the shaikh's chief spy. His Highness was saying quietly: 'This Ernest—he's gone too far.'

Stavridis was silent, for he knew about Ernest. His real name was Ernst and he had come from Switzerland. And, Stavridis had discovered, from other places too. But Stavridis stayed silent. His Highness wasn't talkative but this evening he wanted to talk. Stavridis would let him since he was an accomplished courtier as well as informer-in-chief.

But the shaikh didn't go on at once; he too was thinking of Switzerland. He had been sent to school there and hadn't enjoyed it. The school had been international, outrageously expensive and, in His Highness's opinion, entirely bogus. Well, Switzerland *was* bogus. Four and a half centuries of formal independence and what had emerged was the civilization of the watch, the yodelling club, the numbered bank account. The watches weren't bad but, *pace* elaborate publicity, no better than other watches. And the smugness, the complacency! His school had been thick with foreign princelings and its keynote had been responsibility. For what? For the creatures he ruled? He cordially despised them—coast Arabs half *hubshi*. No, he hadn't liked Switzerland. An exceptionally high standard of unexceptionable mediocrity.

But it had taught him much, though hardly what had been intended; it had taught him above all things caution. One couldn't put the clock back but one could certainly still slow it. So there was a fine modern hospital which British Members of Parliament could enthuse over when they visited the shaikhdom. Their visits, His Highness thought, were tiresomely frequent. And he believed there was even a school—come to think of it he'd opened it. So you bribed, you paid Danegeld. Even in England there was something called surtax.

The shaikh said again: 'This Ernest, my chauffeur. My head mechanic, if you prefer it.'

'He came here from Switzerland.'

'I know he did. I took him on the recommendation of my banker. I keep money in Switzerland, you know.' His Highness looked at Stavridis. 'As I hear you do too.'

Stavridis didn't duck it. 'It's safe there,' he said.

'It used to be safe—now I'm not sure. In any case it was my Swiss banker who suggested Ernest. Perhaps it was something rather more than a recommendation, but I never asked the motives for it. I couldn't. At the time I was more than usually beholden to Werner since he'd just obliged me in a matter which is illegal under my grandfather's stupid Treaty with the British. That's what makes him a successful Swiss banker, just as it would elsewhere. Ernest's a handsome man and Werner has daughters. That was only a guess but it begins to look a good one.' His Highness's surprisingly fair skin flushed. 'He's just made a pass at Madame,' he said. 'He's gone too far.'

Stavridis asked: 'Madame?' It was phrased as a question but wasn't. Stavridis had heard it too. It was his business to hear things.

'Madame, alas.'

She was Shaikh Ali's half-sister and half a Frenchwoman. His father had married her mother in Nice and the princess was unimpeachably legitimate. She had no more claim to the title princess than her brother had to Highness, but the courtesy cost nothing and was expensive to neglect. And she mostly preferred to be called Madame. It was much less pretentious and she was proud of her mother's blood. She lived in a sprawling palace in the city's only park. From the outside it was the usual graceless jumble of coast-Arabic architecture, but the interior was the home of a very French

3

Frenchwoman. There was a flat in Nice too, and a *pied-à-terre* in London. The princess spoke French and English, and beautiful classical Arabic which her father had hired a tutor for and which was almost incomprehensible to the inhabitants of the shaikhdom. She was a woman who lived in three worlds and in any was an ornament.

Stavridis said respectfully: 'And Madame has complained?'

'Far from it. Who ever heard of my sister complaining of male attentions? He's very good-looking, too. *I'm* doing the complaining. My chauffeur——'

'It's an outrage, I agree.' Stavridis spoke smoothly. 'You would like him eliminated?'

'No.'

'If I may ask . . . ?'

'I like the man.'

Stavridis went silent again. He wasn't surprised and he had formed his own opinion. His Highness had his orthodox quota of wives and a proper and seemly complement of ladies of lesser status. And he was childless by all of them. There had been whisperings, shocked noddings of bearded chins. Ernest was a handsome man. . . .

Stavridis for once was wrong. Shaikh Ali was fond of Ernest, but for a reason Stavridis had never guessed. Ernest would beat the shaikh at chess—not could but would. There were perhaps half a dozen men in the kingdom who could give the shaikh a game, but only Ernest beat him. The others played straight till the last dozen moves, then, with His Highness in an impossible position, made some stupid transparent mistake.

His Highness was sick and tired of it. So Ernest drove him by day and played chess with him by night. He was going to miss Ernest, he wouldn't have him killed, but he'd have to give a reason if he vetoed what was obvious; he said to Stavridis: 'I always call him Ernest but his real name is Ernst. His father was a German.'

'What's now an East German.'

4

'What's the difference? But you told me once he was born in Hong Kong, or rather that you suspected it.'

Stavridis nodded.

'Well, there you are. Quite possibly he still has dual nationality, and I can't risk what you call an elimination with a possible British subject.'

'The harbour's very big.'

'And the Political Agent unconscionably officious. No, think again. I pay you to think.'

Stavridis did so. 'We could run him across the border.'

'You'll have to do better than that, you really will. We could run him across the border—yes. But if I'm right that he's a dual he could still complain of it. And then? Of two poor risks I think I'd choose killing him.'

Stavridis considered it; at length he said: 'Why not just sack him? He wouldn't find other work here.'

'Not while I bank with Werner—hide money with him, really. I don't dare offend him.'

'Then somehow persuade him to leave?'

'That's possible. But how?'

'If Your Highness will give me a day to reflect——'

'As it happens I don't need to. I was already considering sending Ernst on a maintenance course to England.'

'For your cars?' the Greek asked.

'All two of them. It's a convenience they're both of the same make, but they're not as new as they used to be.' His Highness smiled softly, his beard almost hiding it. Neighbouring potentates bought fleets of American monsters, changing them annually, driving in cavalcade. Shaikh Ali thought them vulgar, cars and men equally. He kept two English bluebloods and they weren't new by any means, but they had a quality which he respected: they would last. Come to that he respected Ernest. He had always envied courage and Ernest had it. Ernest would beat him at chess.

Stavridis asked doubtfully: 'How long does this course last?'

'Three months.'

5

'Ninety days. And then? If he wants to come back again . . . ? But this decides nothing.'

'Decision—this passion to decide things.' The shaikh walked to the window. He was wearing his robes which he didn't do always, something he thought of privately as native dress. But he was a splendid figure, the Arab stereotype which generations of Englishmen had fallen romantically in love with. The affairs had been disastrous, dangerous to the Arab and destructive to the Englishman. But they hadn't always been unworthy.

With Shaikh Ali the appearance was more than usually deceptive; he said surprisingly: 'I know what you're thinking. You're a Greek, a European of a sort, and these impossible Arabs . . . they'll do anything for time, anything not to grasp a nettle. They're orientals of course. . . .'

'I——'

But the shaikh had sat down again, talking with an irony wholly un-oriental. 'You must forgive me,' he said mildly, 'if I speak with less than courtesy. When you were learning civilized manners I was at school in Switzerland. Sometimes it betrays me.'

'I am here to command.'

The shaikh nearly laughed but managed not to. . . . Command! It was a formula and a senseless one. Nobody commanded, or not if he were wise. You could slow things down, you could watch the dam. And that was all. Orders were meaningless and he wouldn't talk meaninglessly. Instead he said: 'So I've been considering this maintenance course for Ernest and they've agreed. The date isn't fixed yet, but now we'll send him at once. I don't think they'll pack him back because he arrives without formal notice— I fancy it rather flatters them to have foreign and princely chauffeurs. So we'll send him on this course tonight. It's at Derby as it happens and you never see the sun there. Put him on a plane tonight. See that he has money. And when he comes back, *if* he comes back. . . .'

6

'Yes, Your Highness?'

The shaikh said blandly: 'You're to let me know at once.'

Stavridis bowed and withdrew, and Shaikh Ali sent for coffee. He was feeling decidedly low. The evening stretched before him and he didn't know what to do with it. A dozen women awaited him and later he'd go to one of them. But scarcely with gusto. He was a pious man and dutiful; he knew what was expected and he knew he couldn't dodge it. The fact remained that he'd rather be playing chess.

. . . Ernest or maybe Ernst. And quite a man. His Highness was a ruler though it was something he took no joy in, a ruler of Arabs at that, and he was far too experienced to rely on the information which a single official brought him. He maintained his own sources, Stavridis apart, and what he had learnt of Ernest he hadn't disapproved of. Indeed his respect had grown. If Ernest was what they said he was the English might have a handful.

And that was all right too. He'd never much admired them.

Colonel Charles Russell was sitting in his shabbily comfortable room in the Security Executive. He was reading *The Age* and nothing he could have done would have given the observer so misleading an impression of him. Colonel Russell was a part of the establishment, in a special and practical sense one of its props and pillars, but he certainly wasn't of it. To begin with he was an Anglo-Irishman and the English still amused him. He had a sceptical, pragmatic mind and, though he loved his work, he never let it ride him. It was mostly accepted nowadays that the good official was the harassed one: the more paper on his desk, the more obviously he swung between knighthood and nervous breakdown, the better he was, the more eligible for promotion. Russell considered it dangerous rubbish, and in the establishment of his day he was something of a survival.

But his business was security in whatever of its protean forms, and he was obliged to read *The Age*. It wasn't the

7

paper he took at home, its news was unreliable, especially on the foreign page, and its leaders were so woolly as to verge on the merely meaningless. Nevertheless it was a document of Russell's trade. For one thing it would tell him what the establishment was thinking and for another it would tell him what the establishment happened to know. Charles Russell smiled, correcting loose thinking. What *The Age* would really tell him was what the establishment did *not* know.

He settled to the daily chore of degutting his fivepence-worth. It had already been marked for him, but it was a Wednesday, and he would allow himself the luxury of starting on the bridge column. It had always amused him that the stuffiest of newspapers employed the least orthodox of bridge-writers. Charles Russell read his article, playing the hand mentally. He would have bid it very differently and in any normal company he would also have made an overtrick.

He then settled to the leaders. The first was about the shaikhdom, where a Minister of State from the Foreign Office was shortly to pay a visit. Russell read it with distaste. . . . A country still in the Middle Ages but suddenly grown rich on oil. The social pressures. . . . High statesmanship would be called for and the sympathy of enlightened men. The ruler's responsibility (since Shaikh Ali was Highness only by courtesy *The Age* grimly called him ruler) was to guide his people into the new world struggling to be born around them. Britain could help and would. . . .

Charles Russell snorted. Like hell she would. Three-eighths of her oil came down through Shaikh Ali's pipelines.

In any case it was a sea of words: the salt was simpler. Here was an untidy little Arab protectorate. The word might offend the Foreign Office but it perfectly stated the real position. There was a British Political Agent and, somewhere south down the Coast, a personage called the Political Resident. A Knight Grand Cross of the British Empire, a Knight Commander of Saint Michael and Saint George, a natural, therefore, to read *The Age*. And there was a British chief of

8

police who was nominally answerable to the shaikh. Russell's smile broadened, for he had a wide experience of police officers officially responsible to one man, in reality to another. There was something called a police force too, though none of its members was a native of the shaikhdom. That, Russell knew, was the basic danger. There was work in the shaikhdom, work to spare, but it was work which demanded a minimal skill or at least the intelligence to benefit from training. And the subjects of Shaikh Ali weren't notable for intelligence. The oil Terminal was a paradise for minor technicians, but they were Germans and Persians, Sikhs and the stateless men. The inhabitants were helots still; the inhabitants resented it. Shaikh Ali was sitting on dynamite.

Charles Russell warmly sympathized, for he himself had been sitting on dynamite for half a lifetime. And *The Age* said the British could help and would. So God help us all. There was a convention that a despot in a difficulty was best assisted by giving him a constitution (constitutionalizing him—ugh!) so the conventional obeisance had been made to contemporary values. Shaikh Ali was to be presented with a Council. Putting it bluntly, he was going to be forced to accept one. The Council would have an elected majority, but Russell knew too much about the East to suppose that His Highness would be immoderately worried by it. The East didn't work by counting heads, the East had its own old wisdom. Shaikh Ali would know how to handle a Council; he'd make dependent clowns of them and fools of their earnest sponsors. He was much more likely to be worried by George Heldon's imminent visit, for George Heldon was a Minister of State at the Foreign Office, one of the too numerous underlings whom Her Majesty's Principal Secretary of State for Foreign Affairs had recently acquired or had simply had dumped on him. And in Russell's opinion he was unrelievedly a danger. He'd go blundering down to the shaikhdom to inaugurate the Council, making brotherly speeches, drinking too much and dropping clangers. If a man could put his foot in it George Heldon would do so.

It was a pity that the shaikhdom wasn't important enough to rate a visit from the Foreign Secretary himself. Vincent Gale you could do business with. Russell knew a great deal about him but that only increased a mature respect. Vincent Gale you could talk to freely and Russell often did so since they spoke the same language. He was a Foreign Secretary in what was nowadays the slightly suspect tradition that the first duty of a Foreign Secretary was to promote his country's interests. Not those of the league for this and that—his own. He'd have hit it off with Ali, yes indeed. It might even have helped that he knew his sister, that splendid, that magnificent princess. Madame.

If the files were correct, and they mostly were, Madame and Mr. Vincent Gale had been something more than friendly. Russell had met her too. He considered the Foreign Secretary a notably lucky man.

He returned to *The Age* but threw it down angrily. This wasn't its idiom nor even within its knowledge. Come to that it knew nothing—nothing that mattered. It would never, for instance, have heard of a man called Ernst. *Alias* Ernest. And that reminded him: there had been a report on Ernst the previous evening and he'd still to discuss it. He pressed the switch on the intercom, asking for Major Mortimer.

Robert Mortimer came in quietly, taking a chair but not before Russell offered it. He was Russell's assistant, one of three, younger than his master by perhaps ten years. He was tall and severely dressed, and if he spoke deliberately it was not because his mind was slow but because a certain deliberation was the proven foil for Russell. Charles Russell said briefly: 'Ernst.'

'We know surprisingly little about him.'

'I try never to be surprised.'

The byway was tempting but Mortimer resisted it. 'I meant that for an agent of that class—perhaps I should say of that potential—we usually have a pretty complete dossier.'

'We do. Ask us to write down the names of the dozen most dangerous enemy agents and we'd do so. And ten of those twelve would also be on the enemy's own list of his twelve most effective men. We might not get the grading right, but ten names of twelve would coincide.' Russell looked up. 'But we know nothing of this Ernst?'

'Not quite nothing, sir. He's about thirty-six for one thing, and nothing had been heard of him till two years ago. That's unusual for an agent of that age. We've traced him back to East Germany but not behind it. He says he's a refugee from it; he says he escaped and has scars to support it. Then he turns up in Switzerland. The Swiss are severe with refugees. . . .'

'Unless they've got plenty of money.'

'. . . But he somehow found work with a banker called Werner. Who's clean on our records but not on the Bank of England's. Werner recommended him to Shaikh Ali, who banks with Werner's obliging bank. Now why should Werner do that?'

Russell said calmly: 'I guess only when I have to. Assuming this Ernst's an agent, the fact that Werner's clean with us doesn't prove that he's not another. I only wish it did. Or Ernst could have *asked* to move, in which case either Werner's recommendation to Shaikh Ali was innocent—after all there's a banking connection—or else, if Ernst is what we think he is, he may have worked up some hold on Werner. All that is surmise. What's important at the moment is that if Ernst is an agent he wouldn't have gone to the shaikhdom unless he wanted to. So at bottom we're assuming that he did. It isn't the easiest place to get into, especially for refugees, and a job with the shaikh himself would be the perfect cover for any operation.' Russell shook his head. 'So I'm content to leave the how and why, at any rate till they're relevant. What's relevant now is that Ernst was in the shaikhdom. Why?'

'I heard you say "was", sir.'

'You did and were meant to.' Russell rose and unlocked a safe, passing a telegram to Robert Mortimer. 'That came in late last night. It's from Bolton, the policeman. He answers to Ali but not all the time. Part of it he sends me telegrams in G-four-fifty. I approved him for the job and don't regret it.'

Mortimer read the telegram. 'I knew part of this,' he said.

'You knew Ernst had come to England?'

'Yes, but not why.'

Russell didn't comment. It was the first of his considerable virtues that he gave his subordinates a great deal of rope; he didn't insist on knowing everything, since when something important finally broke they'd come to him fast in any case. He asked equably: 'You've a man on him of course?'

'Of course, sir.'

'Good. Then there's a question still between us. Ernst was in the shaikhdom. Why?'

'I've been trying to discover but it's disappointingly general. That shaikhdom must be one of the most sensitive spots on earth. If ever a man was sitting on revolution it's Shaikh Ali. And a first-class agent, an agitator rather than the usual spy or strong-arm——'

'Anarchy,' Russell said; he pulled his moustache. 'An option on anarchy.'

'But who holds the option?'

'I wish I knew.'

'The usual people?'

'Hm . . . maybe. And maybe not.' Russell went matter-of-fact again. 'Meanwhile,' he said crisply, 'this man's in England.' He took the telegram from Mortimer, reading it again. 'Ostensibly doing a course of driving and maintenance at the firm which makes Ali's cars.'

'And lying low. Not a foot out of line yet. Not even a dubious contact. Certainly nothing to link him with our usual friends.'

'Cars,' Russell said. 'At Derby too.'

'I'm not sure I follow, sir.'

Russell said reflectively: 'One of the surest signs of approaching senility is a compulsive suspiciousness.'

Mortimer didn't answer for he'd had plenty of experience of what Russell called his suspiciousness. Mortimer called it second sight and was sometimes a little afraid of it. Its percentage of winners was eerily high. He waited for Russell to speak again and soon Russell did so.

'I was thinking that it's a very well-known motor-car. Lots of V.I.P.s run them.'

'But——'

One of four telephones on Russell's desk rang sharply. He picked it up, then passed it across to Mortimer. 'For you,' he said. He watched Mortimer dispassionately as the telephone quacked noisily, but Mortimer's face was professionally expressionless. Presently he said: 'Wait,' turning again to Russell. 'It's Vincent Gale,' he said. 'The Foreign Secretary.'

'Wanting to talk to us?' Russell looked at the telephone. It was black and an open line. 'On that?' he asked. He sounded shocked. 'Gale talking to us on that?'

'No, it's *about* him.'

'Well?'

'His car has been found in a wood in Berkshire. Wrecked.'

'What make of car?'

Robert Mortimer told him.

'Interesting. And Vincent Gale?'

'Not in the wreck, sir.'

'Blood? Any sign of a struggle?'

Mortimer spoke into the telephone again; when it answered he faced to Russell. 'No blood, sir. Just the wreck.'

'And papers?' Ministers behaved outrageously with papers.

'A briefcase, it seems.'

'Hell.' Charles Russell stood up. 'Who's calling?'

'The local police—I know them well.'

'Then tell them not to touch a thing, tell them you're coming down. Take the Special Branch with you—they've an interest in Ministers' safety. Use my car. Net the radio back to this desk. And move.'

Chapter Two

Vincent Gale had been packing a bag to spend a weekend with his sister in the cottage they shared in Berkshire, humming a tune from a musical which his children, if he had had any, might have been astonished that he had seen and enjoyed four times. Packing was a chore, but he packed with the quick concentration which the Bar had taught him, ready, when the chore was done, to switch his mind smoothly to anything more important or perhaps simply more interesting. The cottage was well placed between the horse-nonsense of Newbury and the deadly propriety of Thames Valley commuterland, and he had bought it with his sister when both had been poor. Vincent Gale was looking forward to his weekend, for he had been working hard and he was fond of his sister. There was a small cloud on the horizon in that George Heldon was coming to lunch on Saturday. He had in effect invited himself, but he was the senior of Gale's assistant Ministers, and though he would probably drink too much he'd go to sleep afterwards. Whilst reasonably sober he'd want to discuss the shaikhdom, and Gale, if his luck held, could perhaps disabuse him of his more dangerous misapprehensions. But more likely he couldn't. Heldon had virtues but judgement wasn't one of them.

Vincent Gale was Foreign Secretary, and it had sometimes

occurred to him that if he had been born one rung upwards in the preposterous English hierarchy he wouldn't have been a Minister at all. Suppose he'd been born to some minor cleric, some country parson with a comfortable College living, or with a private income to blunt his competitive edge. Then a high-minded liberal was what he'd have been, a man in the ageless tradition of being useful to his masters when an appearance of progressiveness was necessary, somebody to be ruthlessly thrown to the wolves in either party's real crises. Gale had seen it happen at least three times, but he'd never been threatened himself. He smiled the smile which his detractors, and they were numerous, thought impersonal and cold-blooded, a jumped-up lawyer's smile. He was a Queen's Counsel, and though he had been a Member of Parliament for fifteen years his Silk wasn't artificial. He could return to the Bar provided he didn't wait too long, and in any case his tastes weren't extravagant. Enough to eat agreeably while avoiding the carbohydrates, enough to indulge a taste for wine. A modest flat at an unfashionable address but a good Scots housekeeper. Presentable clothes though he hadn't many. Theatres and an annual holiday abroad. Enough to amuse an attractive woman. He'd never married.

He shut the bag and brushed his hair. The face that looked back at him didn't look forty-six. Then he telephoned for a taxi. He had five minutes to wait and he might as well use them. Vincent Gale began to think.

He thought about the party, for his position in it wasn't easy. It was in fact dependent on the Prime Minister's sheer need of him. He got on with the Prime Minister extremely well; he even admired him; he particularly admired him that he went to an elocutionist once a week, not, as it was whispered, to improve his speech but expressly to preserve his own. That flat Brummy voice was a political asset and a man was entitled to preserve his political assets. But Vincent Gale spoke proper now, a southern English so effortlessly standard that even judges believed he'd been born to speak it. That, in this England, was a professional advantage. He had professional advantages including an excellent brain, but politically he was a maverick; he wasn't branded Old, Old Guard and he wasn't an intellectual. In both these senses he wasn't in.

But he was—he was Foreign Secretary. And plenty resented it. It had even been necessary to appoint George Heldon as one of his Ministers of State. He was the last man Gale would have chosen but the Prime Minister's first choice, for though the party had won its election it had torn itself to tatters in its victory. It was now an uneasy alliance, short of experience, shorn of competent administrators, the men who could run a department of state, meeting their officials on level terms, telling them in the pinches to go jump in the lake. Vincent Gale could do that and would. There weren't very many who would even consider it.

He rose as the street door-bell rang. His housekeeper appeared from nowhere, a little offended that he'd done his own packing. 'I'll take your bag,' she said.

'It's kind of you but it's much too heavy.'

'Then send down for the taxi-man. Money's too easy in England.'

'Mistress McKay, you're a fascist beast.'

They were very good friends. Edith McKay had the Scot's sound instinct for a considerate master but for Gale she had something more. He could behave like a cold one but he wasn't cold-hearted. When she'd been ill he'd been a great deal more than generous, and he'd given with the easy matter-of-factness which alone made gifts acceptable. She might have been doing him a favour by her misfortune.

Gale picked up his bag. 'I'll be back Sunday evening.'

'Late, I suppose. And good food spoiled again.' She sounded severe but Gale knew she wasn't.

'Would you keep something cold, then?'

He walked down to the taxi, directing it to St. Pancras.

16

He was catching the six fifty-five to Derby where he sent his car annually for a maker's overhaul. He'd pick it up Saturday morning, then drive comfortably down to Berkshire. There was a restaurant car on the train but he wouldn't eat on it: the food would be poor and the service worse. Vincent Gale was conscious that he had colleagues who would consider the thought a serious betrayal. . . . Of what? It wasn't clear. If it had been, if he'd instinctively thought like that, he might have been more popular. He smiled a little wryly. It would have been agreeable to be better liked but not at the price of conditioned thinking. What nonsense the party hacks could talk, how perfectly convey a glum disapproval. His car, for instance—they hated that. As a symbol it was a rich man's perk, though in fact it was eight years old at least and he'd bought it for less than the solid family saloon which would have excited no comment. He'd earned every pound of the modest price he'd paid for it, but that, to the Left of him, wasn't relevant at all. This particular make of motor-car was simply original sin.

Vincent Gale spent the night at the hotel he always went to. It was unfussy but comfortable, for he was of an age to appreciate comfort though not yet to be dependent on it. Then he picked up his car and drove south, watching the stark beauty of the naked February countryside. He drove slowly at first but as the splendid engine warmed his speed, without his knowing it, crept up. It was never excessive, he was an experienced careful driver, but the needle slid up unnoticed. The miles slid away with it.

He was doing perhaps seventy when he realized he had lost control. At first he didn't credit it, then he felt suddenly sick. The steering had gone, the wheel didn't answer. He held it in an unbelief, working it left, then right, feeling for the contact he knew wasn't there. By reflex his foot was off the accelerator but it was discipline which kept his braking light. If he trod on them hard he'd throw her off line, but if she held herself straight till he could ease her down to thirty, twenty. . . . A matter of seconds to live in or not to. The road was straight and empty . . . no, a lorry was coming up at him. . . .

But he'd the ghost of a chance if he kept his head. One of the things he'd ordered was a check on the wheels' alignment. There wasn't a cross-wind and she was heavy and sat down solidly. There was forty on the clock still and it felt like a hundred but the needle was dropping fast. He'd done it or almost. If it weren't for that lorry. . . .

Suddenly she swerved outwards. Gale instinctively put his left down hard, almost falling across the wheel. The lorry swung away from him, missing the berm by inches. He saw nothing but he heard in fear the shouting of an angry man, the sickening crunch of steel. They'd caught his offside fender then, and that would throw him inwards.

And had thrown him too far. Now he braked hard. It was going to be the ditch all right so he might as well check her. He saw it coming up at him, then dived for the floor. He was terrified but thinking still; he wouldn't be pinned by a broken wheel. There was a shattering shock as the bonnet reared, another as the rear wheels took it. A slithering bumping run and something which sounded like timber splintering. Very slowly the car rolled over. Vincent Gale went with her.

He lay for a moment with the nearside door above him. There was a noise of steam and that would be the radiator. The engine would be hot as well, and with a nearly full tank of petrol spilling. . . .

He must get himself out and quick. It wouldn't have been distasteful to do nothing for a bit, letting the world come slowly back, savouring life again. But there wasn't much life in a burning coffin. Gale felt for the door above him. It seemed to have jammed and then it hadn't. He pulled himself shakily out.

Vincent Gale was extremely sick.

When he had finished he felt himself carefully. He was

bruised and badly shaken but nothing seemed broken. He lit a cigarette, careful with the matches. The car hadn't caught and perhaps now it wouldn't. Not that it mattered—the saloon was a wreck. It lay fifteen yards off the road at least, half hidden in a wood. Passing cars might not see it, or they mightn't at once, and Vincent Gale was glad of it. He wanted to think, not answer questions. He was an experienced driver, somehow alive after his first major crash, and he knew where he was for he had often walked this country. His cottage was a mile away and he could always thumb a lift.

Except that he didn't want to. He was fond of his sister but she was a formidable woman. She'd put him to bed and then she'd be silent. She wouldn't upbraid but she'd contrive to make her mind known. . . . A man of his age smashing his car to pieces like a boy in a hotrod. Gale looked at his watch. And Heldon was due for lunch.

This wasn't the moment for the Minister of State.

Well, he knew where he was. Beyond this wood, a mile at most, was another road. It led to a market town and with luck there'd be buses. In the town was a station.

Vincent Gale had begun to walk. He had found a bus and later a train. He had telephoned to his sister from the station. Then he'd gone back to London.

Mrs. McKay hadn't turned a hair. She had recommended whisky and Vincent Gale had used it.

Robert Mortimer arrived at the wreck after seventy minutes' driving which the Special Branch man had openly disapproved of. They were met by an Inspector whom Mortimer had worked with. The policeman said as they climbed from the car: 'I'll relieve your minds on one thing right away. Vincent Gale's in one piece still. He has a cottage a mile away and naturally we telephoned. But so had he. He walked away from that one'—the Inspector nodded at the wreck—'and he went to the station. Then he telephoned to his sister and caught a train to London. We've checked on that too.

His housekeeper says he's shocked and bruised but she's certain he isn't injured. Still, he's sent for a doctor just in case.'

'That's very good news.' Mortimer in turn surveyed the wreck. 'Quite something to walk away from.'

'Yes.' It was light still but getting colder, and the Inspector shivered. 'Now that you're here we'd better run over it. The boot has jammed solid but there's a briefcase as I told you. We haven't touched it except to fish it out for safety. The engine's cold as a stone by now but the place reeks of petrol. We thought it wiser to get it out.'

Mortimer took the briefcase which the Inspector handed him, his heart sinking grimly as he saw it was an official one. He tried the lock. The case was open. Hell.

Inside were two paperbacks, a cheque book, a handful of letters mostly unopened, cigarettes and a bottle of Gevrey-Chambertin. It was the casual impedimenta of a busy man, thrown together hastily into the first thing that offered. Mortimer showed it to the Inspector and the Inspector shrugged.

'There could have been documents and they could have been taken, but on the whole I think not. That wreck was found when the radiator was still steaming. Two commercials found it and they didn't like the look of things. An important-looking car and nobody with it. No body, no blood, but a pile of vomit. So one of them stayed and the other drove off and told us. We got here at the double and the logbook was in the dash. That's how we knew the car was Vincent Gale's. Then we telephoned to the Executive.'

'Which is properly grateful.' Robert Mortimer was looking at the February-sodden ground. 'Any footprints?' he asked.

'Ours and now yours, and the two commercials'. We're checking the commercials, but if they stole documents they were mighty cool afterwards. And one other set of footprints going straight into the wood. And out the other side again, down to the road and station.'

20

'It sounds all right.' Mortimer had begun to return the letters to the briefcase. One had no envelope and he glanced at it indifferently. Suddenly he was staring. It was a car-maker's bill for service and overhaul and it had been receipted in Derby that day. Mortimer looked at the cheque stubs. Yes. . . .

He sat down on a fallen tree a little white. It wasn't fair, it really wasn't! Russell insisted he never guessed—he didn't need to. He had experience backed by a wicked flair. . . . You drove round the country with Special Branch officers trained to efface themselves, you talked to the police about footprints and checking travellers, and Russell sat at his London desk talking in casual parables. 'It's a very well-known motor-car. Lots of V.I.Ps. run them.' Vincent Gale had been one of them and the car had left Derby that morning.

Where a man called Ernest was working on motor-cars.

Robert Mortimer could have laughed or wept. Instead he rose, returning to the Inspector. He had already made his mind up but he always played fair with the police; he showed the Inspector the receipted bill.

'And so?'

'That car has just been overhauled. It must have left Derby this morning.'

'And accepting it did?'

'We've a man of our own in that works already.'

The Inspector stroked his chin. 'Not police work?' he asked.

'Not police work—no.'

The Inspector hesitated, at last said slowly: 'If we can help. . . .'

Mortimer looked at the wreck again. 'Could you get a transporter? Can you put that lot on to it? Just as it is and all of it. And send it back to Derby?'

'If that's what you want. If that's Executive instructions.'

'We'd be more than obliged.'

The Inspector shrugged a second time. He liked Robert Mortimer and he respected the Executive. 'Can do,' he said.

Mortimer shook hands with him, then went back to his car. The Special Branch man was already sitting there. He was concerned with Gale's safety and, once satisfied on that, he wasn't intruding unless he had orders to. But he said to Robert Mortimer: 'Anything interesting?'

'I don't know yet.'

The Special Branch man looked at him, then dropped his eyes quickly. Something was cooking and smoking hot. He knew the signs perfectly.

Sixteen hundred miles to the east two men were apprehensive too. They had very good reason to be so. The room where they sat was warm and bright, but outside the snow fell silently. Up-to-date machinery was clearing it from the enormous square. One man was lean, for a Slav a giant, the other was stout and deceptively amiable. The stout man was saying levelly: 'We simply can't afford it.'

'What?'

'Another major confrontation.'

'But Ernst doesn't work for us. Far from it.'

'Tchah! Do you think we could keep out of it if that Coast went up in flames?'

'I take your point,' the lean man said.

'It would be quite unimportant whose payroll Ernst lived on. It wouldn't even help us that we've quarrelled with his employers. We'd be dragged in willy-nilly.'

'He's a deviationist too.'

'I'm not a political meeting, man.'

'I meant that he thinks, works it out for himself. An orthodox agent never acts without orders.'

The stout man said thoughtfully: 'That's the worst crime in an agent then?'

'Not quite.'

'Then what?'

'An agent who feels is the worst of all.'

The stout man was suddenly interested. 'You think Ernst feels?'

'In a crisis I think he'd feel.'

'Then he's really *extremely* dangerous. To us.'

Chapter Three

At half past ten on Monday morning Vincent Gale was talking to Colonel Charles Russell. He had quite recovered and secretly was a little proud of it; he was forty-six but he wasn't soft yet. Sunday in bed and the quiet but friendly attentions of Edith McKay had, with a little whisky, wholly restored him. Russell had telephoned on Sunday evening, suggesting that a meeting might be fruitful. He had offered, as was proper, to attend the Minister, but Gale had said he would call at the Executive. He wasn't protocol-conscious, he knew that besides being asked for information he had a reasonable chance of receiving some, and experience had taught him that senior officials were a good deal more expansive in the familiar surroundings of their own offices than when haled before some Minister in a room they didn't know. So the Foreign Secretary was calling on the head of the Security Executive. He had officials who would be horrified at what was formally a breach of the proprieties, but he'd never been under officials' thumbs. That was not the least reason he'd been chosen as Foreign Secretary.

He looked round Charles Russell's room as they quickly exchanged the courtesies. There was an open fire, two excellent Persian rugs, a wooden hatstand bent in a complicated pattern and an orderly but unfussy desk. The armchairs were leather, faded but comfortable. Lithographs of Spanish scenes—Roberts, Gale decided, or maybe Lewis—and a generous sideboard which by all accounts held sherry. But it was still too early for that. Russell sat at his desk and he wasn't wasting time, his own or another's; he was saying in his cool clear voice: 'I've a competent assistant who's convinced you were nearly murdered.'

Gale didn't protest and Russell approved it; he asked instead: 'But why?'

'If you'll let me I'll come to that later. May I ask you two questions?'

'Of course.'

'Then you've been sending your car to the makers every year?'

'Every year since I've had her.'

'Was there anything wrong with the steering?'

'No. I ordered an alignment check, but that I do always.'

'Then it's my turn to give.' Russell relit his pipe. 'There's a well-known foreign agent in the works you sent your car to. I say well known but in fact we know less about his background than we'd like. Of course we're trying to remedy that but we do know where he came from.'

'Yes?'

'He came from Shaikh Ali.'

Vincent Gale considered it and Russell watched him. He respected the Foreign Secretary but he wouldn't have sworn he liked him. There was something about him, a certain detachment, on the surface a certain lack. Of course he'd never married. Russell suppressed a smile. He'd never married either; not that he'd lived celibate—no, indeed—but he'd given as well as taken, given happily, whereas from what he knew of Vincent Gale he was a very cool hand indeed. He'd meet obligations but emotions he wouldn't spend. Perhaps if that affair with the princess had really come to anything. . . .

But Russell wouldn't mention that. He wasn't even supposed to know.

But Vincent Gale was speaking again. 'But why should Shaikh Ali kill me?'

'I don't think *he* meant to. This agent's called Ernst or Ernest and was employed as Shaikh Ali's chauffeur. It's been reported that there was what we now learn to call some little local difficulty with one of the shaikh's family, and he dealt with it not by having Ernest knifed or even running him over the frontier but by sending him to England on a three months' driving and maintenance course. He was taking it in the Derby works, and my wholly reliable assistant is convinced he fixed your steering.'

'Can he prove it?' Gale asked.

'Not yet, maybe never. Your car is eight years old at least and even the best steerings fail.'

'Which implies you must show mine didn't.'

Russell was silent. The Minister had spoken with a hint of asperity and Russell didn't blame him. This was a world the Minister might have heard about but he hadn't yet experienced it. Nevertheless Gale seemed interested; he thought, then said reasonably: 'Assuming you were right about my car—repeat assuming—you think this Ernest might have been working for somebody other than Shaikh Ali?'

'As you said yourself, why should Ali want to kill you?'

'You're suggesting the usual people then?'

'No, I'm very far from sure of it.'

'But damn it, who else?'

'I'm in the difficulty that you know much more about the shaikhdom than I do, but let's consider it just the same. Shaikh Ali is sitting on a powder barrel. His subjects, if I can call them that—his people speak Arabic, though not every Arab would be happy to be classed with them. The oil flows across his kingdom and he takes his ten per cent on it. He benefits but who else? Work at the Terminal? But that's for technicians. There's a man of your own called

Political Resident, and in the shaikhdom itself an underling called Agent. And none of that makes jobs for Arab peasants. There's a police force too with a British head, but the men are Sikh mercenaries.' Russell hesitated, weighing the Foreign Secretary; he said at last: 'The place is an anachronism.'

'Agreed,' Gale said calmly. 'It stinks.' He smiled. 'It stinks, but of oil.'

Charles Russell thought carefully. It hadn't been his intention to read his Foreign Secretary a lecture in politics, but Gale didn't seem offended. There was a hint of irritation but clearly it wasn't personal. Vincent Gale was a Minister but he wasn't yet a fool; he was saying with scrupulous fairness: 'All this I accept at once. If there's one place on earth where our enemies could probe us it's the shaikhdom. You say this Ernest's an agent?'

'Yes.'

'Which in this context must mean an agitator?'

'Quite.'

'Then you in no way surprise me that he was fishing in Ali's waters. But thereafter I don't quite follow you. On what you tell me Ernest was openly sent here by Shaikh Ali. Then that leaves us with two hypotheses. The first is that Ali was in it too—in effect that he planned to kill me or at least knew Ernst's intention. But you've told me already you don't believe that. And no more do I. So the second hypothesis is that Ernest came here innocently. Whereupon he finds my car under his hands, whereupon he decides I'd be better dead.' Vincent Gale caught Russell's eye and held it. 'A little quick, don't you think? More than a little sudden.'

Russell said blandly: 'I can't deny it.'

'But does it sound credible?' Gale was perfectly courteous still.

'It isn't a word we use here much. We say "within experience".'

'Then, from your experience, please tell me this. Do agents often act like that? I mean without orders.'

'They're mostly trained not to.'

'I see.' There was a considerable silence before Gale spoke again. 'You're presumably examining that wreck.'

'We are.'

'May I ask how you rate your chances of proving any tampering with it?'

'I rate them extremely thin.'

'You do?' Vincent Gale thought it over; finally he rose. 'Then thank you,' he said pleasantly, 'for what I take as a friendly warning.'

Russell walked to the door with him.

When he had left he poured himself sherry. He didn't resent that the interview had been edged; he wasn't a bully, and the sword-play of words, the things you said and the things you didn't, was something he relished when he met an occasional equal. But lawyers! There was something about them he couldn't take. Their logic was incorruptible but behind they were empty men. Russell was perfectly aware what impression he made on Gale: he would be an experienced, suspicious officer with a good but not quite first-class brain. Russell didn't resent that either, quite to the contrary since Gale's assessment was a real and precise advantage; it let him use gifts which Gale wouldn't even suspect in him. Not that gifts was the proper word: techniques put it better.

Charles Russell drank his sherry, thinking about lawyers and thinking about proof. . . . You took an ageing car to bits and you expected proof of tinkering. You were a fool if you did. A lawyer's idea of proof, a court's—you hadn't a hope in hell of it and honourably he'd said so. He hadn't felt obliged to say much more but that didn't mean the Executive stayed supine. Its plan was simple, a routine really. Mortimer had come up with it almost by reflex and Russell had promptly approved.

And that reminded him—Mortimer himself had gone to Derby. He picked up the telephone but put it down quickly.

He really mustn't interfere, he wasn't a Whitehall brahmin.

Ernest had arrived in Derby conscious of a defeat. His assignment had been the shaikhdom but he couldn't be simply planted there since an unexplained jobless foreigner wouldn't have lasted a week. Instead he'd been told that Shaikh Ali banked in Switzerland, and pretty shady that was since he was supposed to bank in sterling. There were possibilities in that and he was to do what he could with them. So he'd gone for that job with Werner. The banker's youngest daughter had been something more than kind to him and unknowingly she'd helped him; she'd earned him the sack but a great deal more. Werner hadn't wanted a scandal, he'd been terrified in his bourgeois way, and the lightest hint that a job further east wouldn't be unacceptable. . . .

Werner had jumped at it. It had gone smoothly beyond Ernest's hopes or schedule but sometimes the breaks did come. To level up, they'd now turned against him. It was a serious setback to have been obliged to leave the shaikhdom, even if only temporarily. If indeed it was temporary—he wasn't sure. The course he had been dispatched on was a matter of three months, and nothing had been said about his not returning. But though he had been given a generous sum of money for his expenses—suspiciously generous—he hadn't been given a return air ticket. And he was unhappy about his papers. He had a British permit for the course at Derby and a personal letter from the shaikh, but he knew too much about travel documents to suppose that it would necessarily entitle him to re-enter the shaikhdom. They could always stop him if they intended to.

Especially now there had been an imbroglio. And it hadn't been his fault—that hurt. His instructions had been precise, to stir up the maximum trouble in a situation which was evidently about as explosive as it could be. He'd been given *carte blanche* as to ways and means, for he'd been carefully trained and was meticulously indoctrinated, and it had been emphasized that he wasn't a spy. The techniques of spying were entirely different. Blackmail stood high amongst them and for blackmail you needed a hold. That was the theory and Werner the classic ploy, but now he was in the shaikhdom and blackmail was irrelevant. As an agitator he hadn't been interested in compromising the shaikh's half-sister. It would be an unnecessary complication and he hadn't even thought of it. Instead she'd compromised him.

He frowned in frustration, for irony, a Western affectation, didn't appeal to him. It had been one of the rare occasions when Madame went out in the shaikhdom in European clothes. It had been appallingly hot and the princess had wanted air. She had borrowed the open car, sitting in the back with what he supposed was some lady-in-waiting, and they had driven to the only hill for miles. It wasn't really a hill, perhaps three hundred feet, but sometimes there was the faintest breeze, a stirring of the barren air, no more. At the top was a mosque and a view across the harbour—jetties and tanks and the endless ubiquitous piping. The water was polished steel, not blue: he didn't like to look for long even in very dark glasses. He had counted eleven tankers and another coming in.

. . . Oil—wicked oil. A few men lived in a brutish wealth: within a mile a people rotted. This was a good assignment, this he *felt*.

At the top of the hill there was a belvedere below the mosque. Ernest stopped the car there, climbing out quickly to open the passengers' door. He'd never before seen Madame unveiled, and once or twice he'd glanced backwards in the driving mirror. She was certainly a beauty—skin, in this sun, no darker than his own, blue unmistakably European eyes, but an Arab's eyebrows, black and arched strongly. She had the cool bold air of a woman of wealth and for a moment he'd hated her. But she was undeniably attractive. So she could afford to be in those casual clothes which cost a peasant's income for a year. Ernst wasn't indifferent to women nor they to him. He remembered Werner's daughter with a real regret, for now he had a Eurasian in the bazaar. He found her disgusting but she was a tool of his trade, an essential link with the men he'd been able to influence. But Madame was quite another world and Madame had a reputation. Not scandalous—that put it too high by far. Say rather that she knew her mind and that good-looking men were part of it. For an instant he'd wished that his assignment had been different. If he'd been a routine spy he could have answered her smile and would have. He'd seen it in the mirror and it hadn't been lost on him. But he'd looked away quickly. What a wet one she'd think him, or worse.

He opened the door and stood quietly holding it. Madame was taking her time. An elegant high-heeled shoe came out, then some taut and expensive stocking. More stocking, a lot of it. Somewhere above the stocking would be skirt. Somewhere seemed right. Madame said suddenly in English: 'Don't stand there like a dummy, Ernst. Help me out.'

He put out an elbow stiffly but she ignored it. Instead she took his hand. A skirt, belatedly, appeared, another long leg. She stood poised for a moment, then tripped unexpectedly. He caught her by instinct.

Even now he couldn't swear to it. The ground had been rough, her heels preposterous. Not that it mattered now. As he'd held her he'd caught the lady-in-waiting's eyes, reading their message between the slits of the burq'a. It had been open hostility, malice. She'd seen and she'd talk.

Madame said coolly: 'You did that very prettily.' She had walked away with the lady-in-waiting.

And now he was in Derby wasting valuable time; he wasn't even sure he could return to the shaikhdom. His frustration had mounted.

It had ended when his foreman had casually told him that the car he was working on was the British Foreign Secretary's. One emotion had ended but another had replaced it. It was uncertainty, and Ernest wasn't used to it. It had been ground into him remorselessly that the first duty of an operator in any sort of doubt was to refer upwards for further orders. Of course there might be circumstances in which it wasn't possible to refer, but for those there were the precedents. There was a precedent for most things and Ernst had had to learn them. . . . See, when Carlos was in Bolivia—the tin, you'll remember—that looked unprecedented. But was it? No. Carlos remembered that in 1953, in Turkey, that was. . . .

Damn Bolivia, curse the Turks. He was supposed to be in the shaikhdom, stirring up revolution. Instead he was in England and the British Foreign Secretary's car had been given him to service. No precedent fitted that one so he'd have to work on principle. The prospect didn't frighten him —it wasn't as though he were unqualified to think. He'd already been high in the party when they'd selected him for subversion; he was as at home with its dialectic as a theologian with hair-splitting. So one thing was axiomatic and at least he could start from that. Revolution came only from anarchy, not from the sham which the decadent West called progress, and killing a British Foreign Secretary would perhaps be a step to chaos. . . . How big a step? Not a big one, he imagined, since they'd simply appoint another. His superiors would hardly have sent him to England expressly to murder Vincent Gale. On the other hand now he was here, now that an unexpected chance had shown itself, they might not be at all displeased if gratefully he seized it. Moreover there was a link with his assignment in the shaikhdom. The political situation in England had been explained to him, and in terms that the present government was the weakest in a century. It wouldn't fight, it wouldn't defend its interests, even oil. The people was soft and its government softer. Of course there were one or two men who weren't, survivals from an age when England hadn't been simply an American satellite, and the Foreign Secretary was one of them. He'd been mentioned by name—Vincent Gale, a dangerous reactionary.

Ernest had seen it with sudden clarity. Since his superiors' aim was revolution in the shaikhdom any man whose position might allow him to frustrate it and whose character would determine that he tried was at least a worth-while target. Ernest had smiled in quick relief. He gave thanks for established doctrine, the clear thinking it made so simple.

He had returned to the works next morning. He was one of three on the course and each worked on a different car. There was only one foreman between them. Ernest had skill and now he used it.

By the following Monday he was wishing he hadn't. He was worried, which wasn't remarkable. He was meant to be worried. Mortimer's plan had indeed been routine—Ernest's superiors would have approved it since it was Stalinist in its simplicity. *The man who has something to hide will often lead you to it if you scare him.* As a refinement of this elementary but solidly professional thinking, if you couldn't sometimes prove a thing the suspect might prove it for you. That is, if you made him.

Mortimer had worked fast and Ernest was feeling the pressure. To begin with his lodgings had been searched: he knew because he was meant to know, the room had been left a shambles. Then the wreck had come in and a gaffer, not his old one, had led him up to it. . . . He'd been working on that car? He had? But the steering had gone like some mass-produced sardine can. Never seen the like of it. . . . Then they'd taken down the steering with the care of surgeons operating. Men had appeared with cameras and another, a metallurgist. He'd had complicated machinery and the air that he'd known something. Finally there had been a visit from front office. The man in the suit spoke pleasantly enough but he spoke unequivocally.

'You're Mr. Ernest?' Foreign chauffeurs on courses were always Mister.

'I am, sir.'

'Then you probably know that one of the things that car was sent in for was a check on the alignment.'

33

'Yes, sir. I saw it on the schedule but it wasn't on my work ticket.'

'I know it wasn't but I'm obliged to ask you straight.' There was a well-timed pause. 'I'm asking you if you touched it.'

'No, sir, I did not.'

'Very well, Mr. Ernest. But I had to be sure.'

Ernest had been anxious but he hadn't thought of breaking. He broke in the lunch-hour and in a sense unnecessarily, for he had been given a very exaggerated version of the methods of British security. He knew they couldn't arrest at pleasure but he'd been told they could always frame you. And then, once framed. . . .

He'd been told that the bravest broke.

And the affair at lunch-time had been an obvious frame-up. The lunch-break was at twelve o'clock and Ernest had found a pub for it. He went partly for company, it was lonely in Derby, and partly to improve his English. He spoke Cantonese and German, and Arabic they'd taught him, but though the English he'd known was coming back it wasn't yet perfect. So he went to The Bell to better it.

And a drunk in The Bell had tried to pick a quarrel. If he'd really been a drunk, which Ernest at once had doubted. He had knocked Ernest's pint over, slopping it across his own ample stomach. Then he'd complained that Ernest had done it purposely. He'd peeled his coat, making bellicose noises, but Ernest had slipped away. A single blow and presto, the room would be crowded. With police but with agents too —Security Executive. Once they'd got him on any pretext. . . .

He had looked at his hands; he'd been told they were good at hands.

He went back to his lodging, collecting his money and papers. His bag he didn't bother with. He knew there was a plane at six and with luck he'd find a seat on it. Luck—it was something he needed. He'd money for a ticket still but no certainty of landing. If they packed him back he'd had it big. Murder in England. . . . He shivered.

And he still had to get to London. But that bit was easier. There was a car at the works which they'd finished with yesterday. The owner was calling at four o'clock and they'd filled her up with petrol.

Ernest went back to the works by bus. He stole the car quietly and drove away.

He knew when he had gone a mile that the car behind was tailing him. It tailed him very skilfully right up to the Heathrow car park.

Charles Russell valued his reputation as a man who could delegate, but that Monday evening he was fiercely tempted to ring Robert Mortimer. When a phone rang he snatched it hopefully. 'Mortimer,' it said. 'It worked.'

'He's bolted?'

'Yes. We're at London airport—both of us.'

'Do you know where he's bound for?'

'He's bought a ticket for Shaikh Ali's. There are plenty of seats in February.'

'How's he going to get out of England?'

'He seems to have adequate money. Also, presumably, the work permit he came in on. Immigration isn't fussy when a foreigner's going out again. Or not unless we ask, that is.'

'And when he reaches the shaikhdom?'

'God knows. Ali won't take him back, I'm sure. I'm sure he never meant to.'

'You're probably right. . . . Could he bluff his way in?'

'He might if we don't warn them.'

Russell said smoothly: 'No, we needn't do that. Suppose they sent him back again. We've the practical proof we work on here but we've nothing a court would look at. Moreover . . .' His voice tailed away and Mortimer had to prompt him.

'Yes, sir?'

'You said the shaikh won't be wanting him back and I said I thought you're right. So if he does bluff his way in how long will he last?'

'He'd have to go underground, of course.'

'And lock his door at night, I think. And keep strictly away from the harbour. I ask again—how long?'

'Not very long if we happen to be right.'

Russell said admiringly: 'That's a very determined man.' He took the final decision easily. 'Very well, you're to let him go. You're even to help him if he gets into difficulties. Ring me back when he's gone.'

Half an hour later Mortimer telephoned again. 'No trouble, sir. He's through in Departure now.'

Russell said on an escaping breath: 'Then that lets us out.'

He knew as he said it it wasn't true.

Chapter Four

Shaikh Ali was finishing a game of chess with Stavridis, his informer-in-chief. He was more than good enough to realize that he was hopelessly beaten and more than enough experienced to know that within a move or two Stavridis would make some flagrant, some humiliating mistake. The shaikh felt his bile rise as inevitably it came. He would have liked to throw the board in Stavridis' obsequious face, and it wasn't good manners which held his hand. This he knew and deplored. His father would have thrown, his grandfather might have been even more decisive since he'd always carried arms. The shaikh sighed but clapped for coffee. Over it Stavridis said: 'I have news for Your Highness.'

'Yes?' Shaikh Ali spoke acidly but it didn't relieve him. Relief lay in violence and he hadn't the will for it.

'News which Your Highness may find surprising.'

'We'll see,' Ali said.

'I've found out about Ernest. You remember I once told you that I thought he'd been born in Hong Kong? Well, he was. Now I've got the whole story and it cost me much money.'

'Is it a true one?'

'At that price it should be.'

The shaikh looked at Stavridis expressionless. Stavridis was Greek and this was Greek thinking. . . . I paid a lot of money for it, therefore it must be good. Shaikh Ali sucked his spittle but contained it. 'Go on,' he said.

'Ernest was born in Hong Kong in 1929. His father was a German merchant and his mother came from one of the Anglo-Chinese families which have thrived on the island for generations. So he has Chinese blood though he doesn't show much of it. He was twelve when the Japanese came in. Germans were nominally their allies but his father disappeared. So did his mother. But the family was comfortably off, and there was a Chinese nurse devoted to Ernest. She somehow smuggled him back to the mainland where she passed him off as her private bastard. She'd been frugal, as Chinese are, and she'd a good deal of money saved. She had him educated, then set him up as a mechanic.'

'No relations went after him?'

'No, why should they? His father and mother had disappeared, and knowing what happened when the Japanese took over nobody could reasonably suppose that an orphan of twelve would survive it.'

Shaikh Ali said indifferently: 'An interesting story.' He had known some of it already but did not say so. He valued his other sources.

'I assure you it gets more so. Ernest would have been in his early twenties when the revolution came to China. By then he spoke Cantonese as easily as he'd spoken German. He'd been there ten years, he thought like a Chinese, and he'd arrived too young to be politically suspect. The communists left him alone. They shut down his garage but they found him a job in a factory. Competent mechanics were worth their weight in gold. Then they began to take an interest in him and he in them. He joined the party and rose in it. They sent him on courses, steadily more important ones. He learnt fast, he was indoctrinated, he was trusted. I don't know all the details but I do know this.' Stavridis leant forward. He had dreadful teeth and Ali flinched. 'Ernest is an agent, a subversionist, I imagine, since there's no secret here worth spying on.'

'But he came here from Switzerland.'

'He could never have been planted here directly. They started him in Dresden where his father had come from. I don't know what his instructions were—not to begin with—but Dresden was an obvious take-off. But something went wrong there. That doesn't surprise me since there are two sorts of communism, and if the East Germans discovered he was working for the other kind they'd react pretty quickly. As indeed they did. They put him in prison on Russian orders but Ernest escaped. That's where he got his scars. Then he works his way to Switzerland, posing as a refugee from communism. Which I suppose in a sense he was. The rest Your Highness has guessed already. It fits together.'

Ali said approvingly: 'I always knew he had guts.' He stared at Stavridis steadily. 'And he was a really good chess player. I'm going to miss Ernest.'

The Greek hesitated unhappily. 'But I have other and unwelcome news. Your Highness, I——'

'Well?' the shaikh said. He'd heard a good story and he hated an anti-climax.

Stavridis swallowed but got it out. 'Ernest is back here.'

Shaikh Ali's face split suddenly in an enormous and shocking laugh. His teeth flashed whitely, his fine eyes ran. He wiped them and recovered. 'How did this happen?'

'He took an aeroplane from England. Nobody was expecting him, no one had orders to stop him. He was known at the airport as Your Highness's chauffeur. He just walked through.'

'Do you know where he is?'

39

'I do. He's hiding with his mistress in the bazaar.'

'I'd often wondered. . . . What sort of a mistress?'

'She's a Eurasian.'

'An Anglo-Indian?'

'No, Arab-Greek.' Stavridis looked up; he said with an astonishing, a wholly pathetic pride: 'Greek women make the best tarts everywhere.'

Ali wasn't astonished. He knew about Greeks or thought he did. Europe's main culture stemmed from them but somewhere the thread had snapped. Now they were sub-Europeans. The shaikh considered. 'That British policeman Bolton. . . .'

'He knows Ernest's back. Ernest used his own name and was recognized at the airport.'

'Does he know where he is?'

'Not yet.'

'Then you're certainly not to tell him.'

'But Your Highness——'

There was a flash of authority, quite unexpected and for that the more impressive. 'You will do as I say or answer to me personally. Try to think. A British Minister is arriving here next week to open the new Council. Do we want a fuss about foreign agents—next week of all weeks? On top of that a gang of cut-throat Sikhs poking about in the city is the one thing guaranteed to start a riot. Keep an eye on Ernest—contain him till it's safe to act. I'll decide his disposal when these British have gone.' The shaikh stood up. 'I charge you,' he said coldly. 'You may go.'

He sat down as Stavridis left him. He was capable of energy but never of sustaining it. Now he slumped in his chair. All he asked was to be left alone, why couldn't they let him be? This innocent British Minister with ideas about democracy. This half-baked Council. What did they think he'd do with it—hold back the flood? Absurd. You could never send the waters back. . . . Ministers from England and now foreign agents. He resented them equally—

40

meddlers. He wasn't at all his father's son but he'd inherited certain cunnings; he could manage the shaikhdom until, until . . .

He looked at his watch, sighing resignedly. He had an appointment with a lady and he wasn't really keen on it.

Chapter Five

Vincent Gale was thinking about the shaikhdom, more precisely about George Heldon's coming visit to it. He had meant to talk to him at the lunch which his accident had prevented and he had been considering another appointment when Heldon had walked into his room at the Foreign Office. Heldon had talked and Gale had listened. Vincent Gale was good at it, and Heldon was his private ear into a world he wasn't at home in. The Prime Minister in his wisdom had stuck him with George Heldon so he might as well make the most of him. That was politics at its best, or perhaps at its least objectionable.

For Heldon was sixty-five, a stalwart of the party which he had served for forty years, but he was anything but the intellectual whom its new-thinkers would have liked appointed. The new-thinkers detested Vincent Gale, intriguing against him ceaselessly. A weaker Prime Minister might have found it necessary to put one of them in the Foreign Office, but the Prime Minister's first and deadly strength was that there wasn't another visible. So he'd put in George Heldon as Minister of State where he wasn't at all a bad one. Not bright but not a bad one. The late Twenties had scarred him, irreversibly conditioning his thinking; he was as irrelevant to the Sixties as a knight in silver armour but as solidly of the party as the party itself was shaky. So the Prime Minister had been clever again. Gale himself would never have thought of Heldon: the fact remained that he was the perfect counterweight to a suspect soulless lawyer.

And as a colleague he had virtues, the chief of them that he knew things—things which Gale didn't. How people thought, which wasn't how Gale did, above all how they felt; he handled the few papers his officials let him see; and he never interfered. George Heldon had virtues but limitations too. Fortunately he knew them. So did the Foreign Secretary, but Gale wasn't a man to despise another because his brain was inferior. He'd seen far too many first-class brains —his officials', for instance. He even admired what he didn't possess. George Heldon had borne the heat and the burden and he deserved his modest palm. They got on in the office admirably.

But not so well outside it. In the office George Heldon was self-effacing, loyal; but in public he was a disaster. The party was a complicated confederacy whose internal strains and stresses had determined a George Heldon as partner to Vincent Gale, but unhappily that didn't make him competent at international junketings, nor even a presentable figure. He drank and became emotional; he talked wildly and rubbish. Where cool courtesy was called for he was matey; he dropped clangers by the cartload. And Christ, how he drank. Previously it had been tolerable but not since he'd been a Minister. In less than a year he'd gone hopelessly down the hill.

Vincent Gale was worried, for when Heldon had left him he realized it wouldn't do. Not this visit to the shaikhdom. Heldon had seen it with an alarming innocence: the Council was to inaugurate a brand new era. It was not. It would look well in New York, *The Age* would write one of its appreciative leaders, but it was an attempt to buy time and the Cabinet knew it, as did senior officials and politicians

43

everywhere. So you couldn't have it opened in a blaze of well-meaning rhetoric. What was needed was something gracious, calm—something vaguely promissory which promised precisely nothing This was serious business—oil.

And it was useless to hint to Heldon, he was too far gone in drink. Shaikh Ali was orthodox so there wouldn't be booze in public, but Heldon would be staying at the excellent new hotel, and in any case he could always take whisky with him. He'd do that for certain and the results could be incalculable. There was enough in the shaikhdom already which couldn't comfortably be calculated.

Vincent Gale decided on a word with the Permanent Under Secretary. He was the most senior of his officials and Gale didn't rate him highly, but he had an undeniable experience which he used to conceal that he hadn't had an original thought since promotion from Third Secretary. Now he was head of the Foreign Service. Gale explained to him quickly and waited.

'I do see the difficulty.'

'Have you any suggestion?'

A careful, a weighty pause. 'We could brief him very carefully. *Exceptionally* carefully.'

'Haven't we already?'

'Well . . . yes.'

'Anything else occur to you?'

'Well . . . no.'

Vincent Gale said slowly, fishing: 'It's a pity I can't go myself.'

This time the answer came quick and pat. 'The Foreign Secretary in person? But that would offend the whole Coast. Every shaikh would expect the same.' The bald head shook, delivering final judgement. 'It would be quite unprecedented.'

'Then thank you very much.'

The official withdrew. He guarded the arcana of a Department's collective thinking. He was also, Gale thought, an ass beyond redemption.

44

Gale began to think quickly. . . . It was unprecedented certainly, but was it quite impossible? He couldn't just go instead of Heldon: that would be an insult and the Minister of State would properly resent it. He'd be certain to resign and then there'd be a crisis. The Prime Minister wouldn't like it, indeed he wouldn't stand for it. Gale walked to the window, looking across St. James's Park. . . . But could he go too—as well? George Heldon could make his speech as planned but at least he'd be there as longstop. People would be watching him. He'd smile at the absurder bits, look deprecatory if it got really wild. He was skilled at looking deprecatory. And if anything too dreadful broke he'd be there to pick the bits up. This was really important, an industrial society's fuel. He'd have to speak to the Prime Minister and he'd need an excuse, a pretext. It would have to be a good one too, but the Prime Minister wouldn't veto what could be shown to be solid sense. The Prime Minister knew about Heldon; he wouldn't admit his own embarrassment but in private he'd be relieved.

. . . Private—a private visit. He could go there entirely privately but he'd still be Foreign Secretary. They'd have to ask him to the opening, that dangerous banquet before it. He could slip in the bland, the deflating word, and if anything went really wrong, some half-baked promise or fatal phrase. . . . They could go on different aircraft, different dates, emphasizing in every way that they weren't an official team. It might be done. It could.

It could, that is, if there was anyone in the shaikhdom who could conceivably be inviting Mr. Vincent Gale on a credible private visit.

Gale returned to his desk. He'd never yet asked a woman to take him back. Not even a princess.

He thought of Madame with acute regret. It had been sudden and urgent and wholly as he liked it. Except that it had ended far too soon. He had met her at a reception, noticing her across a stuffy room. He had known who she was and hadn't bothered with introductions. He had worked his way across the crowd, knowing that she was watching him. He bowed.

'I'm Vincent Gale.'

'I've heard of you,' she said coolly.

'And I of you.'

'You didn't say that very well. You said nothing but much too much.'

He looked at her, considering. Polite denial would sink him flat, she wasn't one to fool with. 'Does it matter?' he asked.

'To me—not at all.' She smiled at him. 'And how do you answer that?'

'I don't even try to.'

'Good.' She looked him calmly up and down. 'So you're Her Majesty's Foreign Secretary.'

'Not all the time.'

'I'm Princess Nahid whose oil you burn. But not all the time. And I don't think I like you at all.'

'That might not be important.'

'Let's say it's irrelevant.'

'You choose the word.'

Twenty minutes later they had been dining together quietly, and by midnight in her London *pied-à-terre*. It had been the most exciting and, in its savage way, the most fulfilling affair of his life. But it had ended sourly and it hadn't been his fault. They had been dining again, and unexpectedly a young man was standing at their table. It was Gale's senior private secretary, and under the smoothly professional manner he was evidently in a most unprofessional tizzy. 'I'm sorry,' he said, 'to disturb you. They told me at your flat that you'd be here.'

'You know Princess Nahid? Sit down at least.'

The young man bowed. 'I don't think I should. It's really very urgent or I wouldn't be intruding.'

Vincent Gale considered it. He knew what it was or could

46

guess with some accuracy. In which case it was undeniably important. On the other hand Madame was leaving for Nice tomorrow—no interruption could have been timed more disastrously. He wavered but decided. He knew that he'd had a predecessor who in similar circumstances would have dealt with the young man summarily. Courteously but unequivocally he would have said it could wait till morning. But Gale had loathed his predecessor. By God, he'd been incompetent, he'd left his country rocky. Not duty then—the word was too big, too pompous: instead it was a grim contempt—what that half-wit would do he couldn't. He said at last: 'I'll take the Princess home, then come.'

'No, put me in a taxi.'

'I'll take you home.'

'You will not,' she said, 'you won't indeed.' She looked up at him, the strong black eyebrows arching. 'I know,' she said, 'you're a busy man.'

He had put her in a taxi and next morning he'd telephoned; he had telephoned twice to Nice and she'd answered most politely.

Now he put on his hat and walked to the Whitehall post office. He sent a long cable, then took a taxi to a florist. . . . Two dozen red roses, and they were to be put on the evening flight. He produced his card, noting with an amused distaste that the girl was at once obsequious. She gave him a bill and he paid in cash. It was a good deal of money and Gale wasn't rich, but he paid without question, thinking that his predecessor, wealthy by inheritance, would probably have charged it to the *frais*. After all this was business. A sort of business.

The girl asked him about delivery but he said he'd fix that himself. Just make sure they were on the evening flight, the crew would be expecting them. . . . He'd ring the airline from the office, that was always more impressive. The Foreign Secretary would be greatly obliged if a stewardess would be good enough to deliver the flowers in person.

They'd do that for the Foreign Secretary but never for Vincent Gale.

In his flat next day at lunch time he was looking at an answer. Madame had been enchanted with the flowers. Roses—he remembered that? At least that was something. As for the rest she'd be really delighted. How kind of him to think of her. (If there was irony the outrageously expensive telegram concealed it.) The shaikhdom could be extremely dull, old friends were always welcome. There was a new hotel, not exactly the Negresco, but it was reputed to be habitable. If he'd signal his arrival arrangements would be made for him. Naturally as her guest.

It would do, he decided—it would just about do. There could be circumstances in which a British Prime Minister might be less than delighted that his Foreign Secretary had been fishing an invitation from an oil shaikh's sister. This wasn't one of them and for an excellent reason. The reason was called George Heldon.

Vincent pocketed his telegram, then rang for his secretary. He was to arrange an appointment with the Prime Minister, and early.

In the cosy well-lit room with the snow outside the stout man was saying with his deceptive amiability: 'Trying to kill a British Foreign Minister is the most idiotic operation ever heard of. Nobody but an oriental would even think of it.'

'He isn't wholly an oriental.'

'Ernest or Ernst? I know he's not. But he's oriental-trained. And you know what they are—damned doctrinaires.'

The lean man said reflectively: 'What I find interesting is not that we know of this but how.'

'You mean that it didn't reach us from our own British sources?'

'I mean just that. There was an accident to the Foreign Secretary's car. That's been in the English papers, but no

48

suggestion that it wasn't an accident.' The lean man tapped a file. 'What we've got here is a deliberate leak. A deliberate leak and expressly to us.'

'From the Security Executive?'

'I'm convinced of it.'

The stout man considered. 'It does make a sort of modern sense. Here's this Ernest in England and he tries to kill Vincent Gale. Russell would be certain we hadn't planned that—he's not a fool and he knows that we're not. So there's only one country which Ernst could be working for.'

'Russell would see it like that, I think. But why leak to us?'

The stout man polished gold-rimmed glasses. 'Because we've an interest in common. This isn't nineteen forty-eight, so consider that shaikhdom dispassionately. Great Britain needs the oil—we don't. We can't use their oil, but equally if there was a revolution we haven't yet reached the stage where we could afford to sit back quietly and see it smashed. Principle apart, there's the question of face—face as against our oriental friends. Who have none of our inhibitions. So we no more want trouble on that intolerable Coast than Russell does.' The stout man pointed at the top paper on the file. 'This,' he said crisply, 'is bait.'

'Colonel Russell expects a *quid pro quo*?'

'Of course.'

'Then what do we do?'

The stout man said unhesitatingly: 'We give it him. And I can guess what he wants, which is simply Ernest's record. He knows almost as much about our own top agents as we know ourselves and has correctly deduced that Ernst isn't ours at all. Moreover Ernst's a *new* one. He turns up in East Germany and there we got on to him. Whether Russell knows that I couldn't say, but I'm certain he realizes that Ernst is none of ours. So knowing our relationship with our dear friends further east there'd be a fair chance we'd play with him. All right then, we will.' The stout man thought again. 'Photograph that file,' he said, 'the bits that matter.

49

After all there's a recent precedent with the Americans. And throw in a good translation for the look of it. You know where to drop it?'

'The usual place?'

'By no means—use your head. This is open—fraternal courtesy. Put on a uniform, use the front door.' The stout man grinned. 'And watch it,' he said, 'the whisky's excellent.'

Colonel Charles Russell was looking at two documents, both of them, in their different ways, triumphs for the Executive. The first was an abstract of private telegrams sent and received by Her Majesty's Principal Secretary of State for Foreign Affairs. Not copies but an abstract. The arrangement had been made when the most likely Foreign Secretary had seemed a man whom Russell knew to be more dangerous than any deliberate traitor, and on Vincent Gale's appointment he had very nearly cancelled it. But it worked and you never knew. He was perfectly aware that possession of this paper would, if discovered, cost him his job in hours, but he had spent half a lifetime in work where to do it properly he must be ready to see his head drop. And never to complain of it. He knew the law, he respected the law, but he bent it unhesitatingly when his country's interests dictated.

The other paper he was prouder of, since he had set a sprat and a whale had returned to him. It was a photocopy of a Russian file complete with an admirable translation; it was the dossier of a man called Ernst, extracted, Russell presumed, whilst he'd been held in a Dresden prison. Extracted—that was the probable word. Russell preferred not to think about the methods.

He sent for Robert Mortimer, smoking quietly while Mortimer read. Mortimer said when he had finished: 'There's a lot we shall have to examine later, but just for the moment two things seem urgent. First, Vincent Gale is going to the shaikhdom. Second, Ernst has just returned there.'

'Which rather upsets our friendly plan to let Ali deal with

him quietly. I still think he will but he may take too long for us.'

Mortimer noticed the 'our' but let it pass. 'Then we ought to warn Vincent Gale?'

'You think that's a good idea?'

'I know it's not brilliant.'

'I think it's excellent in principle but useless in practice. What could we tell him that we haven't already? And he was properly sceptical when I spoke to him before.' Russell prided himself that he was fair-minded when the luxury was permissible, and now he explained the adverb. 'I say properly because he's a lawyer and I hadn't a shred of proof.'

'We could offer that now.'

'But could we? Suppose I talk to him again. If I use the proof he'll be after me like a knife. So what do I say? I must say there was a foreigner in this country whom the Executive deliberately frightened. Major Mortimer had his room searched, he staged an unnecessarily ominous post-mortem on the wreck of Gale's car, and he put on a man to pick a flagrant quarrel in a bar. So the foreigner bolts for it. Accepting what you and I accept that's proof as we understand it but I doubt if it's proof as Gale does. He'd say something about "after it therefore because of it".' Russell laughed without amusement. '*Post hoc ergo propter hoc* I believe is the lawyer's jargon. Gale's very much a lawyer still.'

'Then we could show him that Russian file.'

'We could, I suppose, but we'd never get another if we did and they learnt we'd done so. That file is strictly from one professional to another. We can use the knowledge—obviously we're meant to—but we mustn't expose the source.' Russell was suddenly thoughtful. 'Besides,' he said, 'do we really want to stop Gale's visit to the shaikhdom?'

'That depends why he's going.'

'I doubt if it's merely to see Madame again. That affair was rather a splendid thing but it was six months ago at least. And she has a flat in Nice and another in London—four months of the year is the most she tolerates in the shaikhdom. Gale isn't a boy, so why not wait? So there must be other reasons. I can think of several but all are guesses. What we know is three things.' Russell began to check them off. 'First that the shaikhdom's extremely hot politically—if an explosion is likely anywhere it could come in Shaikh Ali's most easily. Secondly that we need that oil. And thirdly that Gale is a competent Foreign Secretary. He isn't a man to sit in Whitehall if he could somehow serve our interests by a trip to Shaikh Ali's.'

'Which returns us to Ernest, now back in the shaikhdom.'

'Quite. Where we've a man called Geoffrey Bolton. If he thinks we dumped Gale's failed-murderer back on him knowing that Gale was following he'll be furious and rightly.' Charles Russell thought again. 'Will he know Ernst is back?'

'If he doesn't he soon will. He doesn't miss much locally.'

'But he won't know about Gale unless we tell him?'

'He'll hear, I dare say, but he'll need every hour possible for his precautions.'

Charles Russell shook his head. 'It simply isn't good enough. Bolton's a first-class officer who keeps his ear to the ground as well; he sends us valuable information but he isn't Executive-trained. We could leave it at warning him that Gale may be in danger again, but if anything went wrong Bolton would promptly be broken. The man on the spot is the automatic can-carrier. He could also say, and justly, that we'd wickedly double-crossed him.'

Robert Mortimer smiled for he knew the form. 'Would you like me to go down there, sir?'

'I was lumbering towards that one.'

'Very good, sir. Then what's the time-table?'

Russell looked at a note. 'Today is Thursday, and the opening of this Council is fixed for Monday evening. Everything's in the evening there, it's far too hot by day. Heldon is scheduled to leave on Sunday, sleeping the night there, doing his stuff on Monday and returning to England Tuesday.

Gale's flying separately and two days ahead of him. That will be Friday—tomorrow.'

'Then I'd better leave tonight.'

Russell looked at his watch. 'You'll be pressed to make the flight. I'll ring them if that will help you, though. And clothes?'

'I'll buy some there or borrow from Bolton. I'll warn him I'm coming.'

'Good.' As Mortimer rose Charles Russell said: 'I see you take this seriously.'

Robert Mortimer pointed a long finger at the photo-file. '*They* do,' he said grimly. 'That's enough.'

Chapter Six

As the door of the aircraft opened next morning the heat struck Robert Mortimer a blow which stopped him dead. He gasped, his lungs protesting, then walked down the gangway, a hand on the rail. It was barely ten but the tarmac was soft already, clinging hungrily to his heavy shoes. He was carrying his coat and waistcoat but in ten seconds was sweating miserably into inappropriate English underclothes. The sky was a livid, a merciless dome, the air had been breathed by a million men. Who clearly had rejected it. Beyond the fence of the airport the earth swooned interminably, not sand and its wild mad beauty, but camel scrub scarred by some saline excrescence. There wasn't a tree in sight. Mortimer decided he'd been in worse places but only because he'd been under fire.

Geoffrey Bolton greeted him, shaking hands firmly. They had met before and had got on well. Mortimer knew that there were two sorts of British policeman still holding jobs in anomalous corners of what had once been an empire. One was the survivals from the colonial police services, boys taken from school at seventeen, thrust into some police college, and conditioned rather more savagely than the most Pavlovian of dogs. Then they had spent anything from five to twenty years in what Mortimer thought of privately as wog-bashing and, when the wogs at last got rid of them, had fastened themselves on peoples even less well equipped to resist their burden. Where they had been unrelievedly a disaster, especially those from the Indian Police. That was one kind of British policeman still abroad, but Bolton wasn't one of them. He had pounded a beat and was entirely a professional. He asked with a kind of friendly malice: 'Hot?'

'Hot as hell.'

'You're not supposed to be hot at all. This is February—winter, you know. You'll need proper clothes, though. We'll go back to my bungalow and I'll lend you some to go on with. When you've eaten and tidied up a bit I'll take you across to the Terminal. There are shops in the town but a better one there. I'll ring them and fix to sell to you.'

They drove straight to what Bolton called his bungalow. It was in fact a ramshackle old house at the farthest end of what had once been the harbour. There were piers still and Arab dhows, but now the anchorage was a backwater, superseded by the enormous oil port two miles to the north-west. Between the two lay the town, and Bolton began to speak of it. It hadn't changed for centuries except for a single street. Ali's father had carved it from the jungle of slum, a monstrous concrete avenue sixty yards wide and in the style of between-wars functional. Here were the banks, a European shop or two, the hospital and the show-piece school. There were also the new hotel and the houses of the very few who had benefited from the oil which flowed across their country. The avenue began at the sea, starting from the centre of the hundred yards of squalor which had been christened the Promenade. By day this strip was entirely grim but in the evening, when there was a moon perhaps, a breath of reluctant air, it had its own fey charm. There were date palms and arecas too, oleanders in broken tubs, and a couple of band kiosks, iron and still elegant, imported from heaven knew what forgotten Edwardian exhibition. Sometimes a British cruiser would land a band, and astonished locals would stare a whole performance out, giggling at the barbarian cacophony. Bolton explained that in the evening they would go there since they would certainly have to visit the avenue's other end. This was the square and it was very grand indeed. One whole side was Ali's palace and his father had intended wings to fill two others. That hadn't come off and just as well, for there was nowhere else for offices without further destruction in a city already sickeningly overcrowded. So one side was now the offices of His Highness's government and the other, just completed, had been designed as the Council chamber. But walk twenty yards off the concrete and you walked back through the centuries.

Mortimer had listened before asking a question. . . . And the employees of the Terminal, the foreigners, the hated? They lived on their work and Bolton thanked God for it. If they'd lived in the city he couldn't have coped. They had their own shops and houses, water and light duplicated, air-conditioning and a sports ground, clubs according to their hierarchy and above all a wire fence round them. At night it was floodlit. Bolton's writ ran there but only just, since they settled their own difficulties, sending trouble-makers smoothly home. They were a mile to the west of the city proper; they might have been three thousand. They were polyglot and all had skills. Persian, Armenian, Spaniard, Pole—they all had their separate trades. Their isolation made police work easier, but of course things couldn't last like that. Sooner or later there was going to be God's own reckoning, and when the bill was presented. . . .

Robert Mortimer would have been interested in Bolton's ideas of God's own reckoning, but they had arrived at his house. Mortimer could never sleep on planes and he climbed from the car stiffly. Bolton took him to his room. 'Bath first, I suggest, but I'll send you some coffee. You're about my size so I'll send some clothes too. We'll think about buying later.' He smiled his friendly but faintly sardonic smile. 'I see you started luggage-less. That means it's urgent. And I've had your cable. We'll talk when you're ready. Will eggs and tinned bacon suit you? I can't recommend the other sort unless you want a tapeworm. I should add I've a Christian cook.'

'Is that important?'

'To me it is. An old-fashioned Moslem might spit on the bacon first.'

They ate a cross between lunch and breakfast on the wide veranda overlooking the crumbling jetties, the sullen sea. Robert Mortimer, whose profession had imposed on him a necessary optimism, could imagine the faintest stirrings of the ancient lifeless air. Over the last of the meal Bolton said: 'You'd better start.'

Mortimer did so and Bolton listened; he listened for some time. At the end he whistled softly. 'That puts Ernest in Class One,' he said. 'I didn't know that, and since I like to sleep at nights I'm very glad I didn't. The most favoured rumour locally was that his relations with the shaikh were, shall we say? irregular, but knowing Shaikh Ali I never quite believed it. I thought Ernest was a queer one but not a queer. Now you tell me he's a subversionist with a sideline in murder.' Bolton bowed with a friendly irony. 'Welcome,' he said, 'I'm delighted to see you.'

'I don't doubt you'd have coped alone.'

'*I* do. You know my position here. Formally I'm an employee of Shaikh Ali, but if I fell out with the Resident down the coast I don't imagine I'd last an hour. There's an Agent lives locally but he's subordinate to the Resident. I hardly ever see him and I don't complain of that. He's very much Foreign Office second eleven and you know just how second that can be. And he doesn't affect the real position, which is that though I'm technically head of the police what I really command is an army of occupation in disguise. There is something called a police levy but in practice they're

Ali's retainers. They police the town in an offbeat way, which is something I cannot. Or only in emergency. My own men can enter it, but only in bodies, armed. If a sergeant and a constable went chasing a suspect there one of two things would happen: either they wouldn't come out again or else there'd be a riot."

'Sikhs,' Mortimer said.

'Two hundred and four, full strength.'

Robert Mortimer didn't comment. Sikhs were a race with a martial reputation but Mortimer had his reservations. He'd seen them fight and he'd seen them run shamelessly. And they weren't easy men to handle, though Bolton knew the secret. Which was to allow them eight hours' sleep at most and to work them like donkeys the other sixteen. Give them generous leave on generous allowances but never a minute for the intrigue which eternally damned them.

And of course keep them out of the natives' hair. They weren't notable for discretion, tact wasn't their forte.

But Bolton was talking again. 'So what I am in practice is a sort of British presence, and since under the Treaty we can't put in troops unless Ali asks for them I dare say we do a job. But you'll have realized that I haven't the power to pull in Ernest. He may be holed up in the bazaar or'—Bolton waved at the harbour—'he could be hiding in one of those dhows. I haven't had orders to find him, and if I had I'd think pretty hard before I carried them out too seriously. But Ali's no fool where the locals are concerned. This ridiculous state is going up in flames one day, but he's not going to touch it off by ordering me to comb a Moslem city with a gang of unbelievers. He'll know Ernest is back but he also knows that this Council is due to be opened on Monday. The last thing he'll want is the risk of trouble. So he'll play for time as he mostly does; he won't give me orders for Ernest's arrest but he'll tell his own people to find him and watch. Later he'll have him dealt with as you thought.'

'But will that work for us—now?'

'Who knows? According to your rather surprising informants Ernest is pretty competent, and a man who speaks Arabic as he does can disappear in a native city. I dare say they could find him—once—but he could slip them quite easily.'

'Which doesn't look good for Vincent Gale.'

'That's why I'm glad to see you.'

Robert Mortimer considered, feeling his way on to delicate ground; finally he said casually: 'In theory Gale's coming on a perfectly private visit to the princess.'

'And you doubt if that's all the story? So do I. But there won't be complications with the princess. Madame's a woman who has seldom put a foot wrong. With Ernest perhaps, but that was quite exceptional. She must have been exceptionally bored. In Europe she behaves like a rich and sophisticated European but here she lives in a broken-down Arab palace surrounded by women attendants. I'm told there are even eunuchs, though that I couldn't swear to. I'm not on Madame's list, you see, much as I'd enjoy it. In France she goes to Mass, they say, but here she wears a burq'a. There are rooms reserved for Gale in the hotel, on Madame's orders at that, but if he thinks he can walk straight back into any favours she may have shown him, well, there's a big surprise coming to him.'

'He's arriving just the same.'

'Bringing us back to his safety. And I've another worry too.'

'You're earning your money.'

'He's a man called Stavridis, a Greek and not a nice one. He's also Ali's spy-in-chief. And other things.'

'Ali runs his own spy corps?'

'Of course. He's an Arab and so are the locals. Of a sort. Stavridis spies on me and I on him. This, for instance.' Bolton felt in the pocket of his bush shirt, passing a paper to Mortimer.

THIRTEEN FIVE ZERO ZERO AND ZERO ZERO ZERO STOP TWENTY
SEVEN STOP TWELVE SEVEN FIVE ZERO AND ZERO ZERO ZERO
STOP TWENTY SIX STOP NINE SEVEN FIVE ZERO AND ZERO ZERO
ZERO STOP TWENTY NINE STOP ENDS ACK.

Mortimer reflected. 'I'm not a code man myself but I could probably get it broken.'

'But I don't think it's really code. Look, I've written it out differently on the other side.'

Mortimer turned the paper over.

13,500,000	27
12,750,000	26
9,750,000	29
36,000,000	

'You see what I mean?'

'I'm afraid I don't.'

'My guess is this though it *is* a guess. The two-digit numerals *are* code, meaning in this case that they've a pre-determined meaning we don't know. The rest, I suggest, is straightforward sums of money. Now look at the address.'

Mortimer did so, his eyebrows rising. 'Zürich,' he said. 'There are banks in Zürich, queer ones.' The eyebrows came down in a puzzled frown. 'Lavaterstrasse, 1074. But I know my Zürich pretty well and that's down in Enge. And not in the banking quarter.'

'A cover address?'

'Could be.'

Bolton said with an unaccustomed emphasis: 'It's common knowledge in the shaikhdom that Ali keeps a nest-egg in Switzerland and that under the Treaty he isn't supposed to. The two-digit numerals could be agreed instructions for dealing with the sums of money opposite. Twenty-seven

60

might mean transfer to New York—Ali banks in Switzerland but loathes it, he'd never settle there—or sell Montecatini or even buy I.C.I., though British Blue Chips aren't popular with oil shaikhs. That's guessing again but I can tell you two things more. They're that I've seen cables like this before, but never before those particular two digits.'

'That makes it more interesting.' Mortimer thought again. 'You say Stavridis sent this telegram, not Ali?'

'Yes. Stavridis has money in Zürich too, but thirty-six million francs is much too big a sum for him. In any case I told you that he did other things for Ali besides spying for him.'

Robert Mortimer did some mental arithmetic. 'Thirty-six million francs,' he said. 'That's three million pounds. Do you think an oil shaikh could live modestly on three millions?'

'I really don't know. He might if he economized.'

'Have you ever had sums like this before? Millions of francs?'

'Never. The ordinary telegram was for half a million or so—orders to sell or buy, I'd guess.'

'So that this could be something bigger? Ali could be making his—well, his dispositions?'

'Let's say that the sums suggest it.'

There was a long silence before Mortimer said slowly: 'Suppose he did run while the going was good.'

'I'd much prefer not to.'

'That would blow this place wide open?'

'To the skies,' Bolton said.

Chapter Seven

There was a day-time plane on Fridays and Vincent Gale had travelled on it. It had been three hours late for no evident reason but Gale had been warned that three hours' delay could, with this clumsy Corporation, be regarded as dead on time. In any case he did not care; he was without engagements that evening, and without an engagement six o'clock was a dreadful time to arrive in any hotel. Instead it was nine and he went straight to his room. In fact it was what the manager called a suite—bedroom and sitting-room and a bathroom with elaborate American plumbing which, in Arab hands, had mostly stopped working a month after installation. There were fresh flowers in the sitting-room but not, he saw, roses. There wasn't a note nor a message with the porter. He ate, not well, and went to bed.

Next morning he telephoned to his hostess's house, surprised that he couldn't contact her. A man's voice had answered first, a carefully-controlled tenor which had run in excitement into an astonishing alto. And the voice's owner had seemed unreasonably agitated. But he spoke no English and little French, and presently a woman had replaced him. . . Mr. Vincent Gale? Yes, naturally he was expected. His rooms were as he wished them? Good. And the princess? he asked. There was a long shocked silence. The princess would no doubt be getting in touch with Mr. Gale.

The woman rang off.

Gale shaved and drank his coffee, then telephoned for a car. No, not to go to the Terminal. He intended to pay his respects to the princess.

Five minutes later the Lebanese manager announced himself. He was bland as became his trade but he wasn't quite at ease. 'Good morning, sir. If I could have a word.'

'By all means. Please sit down.'

The manager composed himself, plump hands on plumper knees. 'If you'd forgive a question, sir.'

'I might.'

'It's a risk I must take. . . . Have you visited this shaikhdom before?'

'No, never.'

'Or any Arab country?'

'I've been in Egypt. If you call that an Arab country.'

The Lebanese smiled. 'I'm a Christian from Beirut so I'll gladly let that pass. And it tells me you're far from ignorant. What I'm less sure about is whether you realize just how backward this shaikhdom is.'

'Meaning?' Gale asked.

'Meaning, if I may say so sir, that you can't possibly make the first move. You mustn't call on Madame uninvited. For one thing she might not admit you and for another it would be a *gaucherie* on your part. An—an ignorance.'

'She invited me here, you know.'

The manager bowed. 'We're honoured to welcome her guest.' He slid quick eyes round the comfortable room. 'But you mustn't imagine this is typical of the shaikhdom.'

'I arrived in the dark but I'd already guessed that.' Gale inspected the manager. He wasn't an impressive man but he seemed to be trying to help. Vincent Gale asked at length: 'Then what do you advise?'

'Frankly, you should wait till Madame contacts you. That's protocol.'

It was a word Vincent Gale had heard before and he knew its grim authority. This was a disappointment but the manager wouldn't be fooling. Gale said on a sigh: 'Then thank you for warning me.'

He settled to wait reluctantly. He had nothing to do but call on the local bigwigs, George Heldon wasn't due till Sunday evening, and Gale was conscious that he was easily bored. He would in fact have been bored to death if a Major Robert Mortimer hadn't discreetly presented himself. Mortimer had seen no reason for subterfuge: on the contrary he had openly introduced himself as an officer of the Security Executive who had been sent to the shaikhdom in the interests of the Foreign Secretary's safety. At another time Gale might have been irritated, but now he was alone and bored and Mortimer was personable. He was rather too old for Gale's idea of a bodyguard, and he had an air of quiet authority which told Gale unmistakably that physically guarding persons in danger wasn't his normal work. Gale asked him mischievously: 'Do you carry a gun?'

'If I do I'm not telling.'

'But you want to stick close to me?'

'If I may. And until you get bored with it.'

'You run the risk of boredom, not myself.' Gale's good humour was returning. This congenial bodyguard was a real stroke of fortune. 'I've one or two formal calls to make, so come along too. I've sent for a car.'

'I suggest we use mine.'

'Armour and machine guns?'

'Not so you'd notice them.'

They drove away in the open four-seater. Mortimer sat in front with the Sikh driver and Gale with another behind. The Sikhs' pugarees were immaculate, their beards wound on strings. They looked noble and rather stupid; they had pistols in holsters but no air that they wished to draw them.

Mortimer was talking to the driver in such kitchen Hindi as he remembered. It was execrable but the Sikh seemed absurdly pleased. They drove round on their duty calls, but sticking to the coastal road and the avenue in the centre. Gale wrote his name in Shaikh Ali's book but not his designation: it was Heldon coming officially—his superior mustn't steal his sun. He left a card on the Agent and drove to the Terminal, calling on the Resident Director. The Director, a little tentatively, suggested that he might spend Sunday on a visit of inspection. There was so much to see. After a quick glance at Mortimer Gale accepted gratefully. . . . Perhaps the invitation would include Major Mortimer?

By dinner on Sunday Gale had realized he'd been enjoying himself. There'd been nothing from Madame but Madame was a woman. He shrugged, aware that the gesture was an over-compensation. The hook was still in but he'd try not to fight it.

He was eating a sodden savoury when he realized there was a disturbance, a discreet disturbance but something to notice still. He looked up at George Heldon. The manager was leading him in, supporting him to his table. He was drunk though not uproariously, but he'd taken a skinful. He didn't notice Vincent Gale but Gale heard him call for whisky. A waiter took the order and the manager spoke sideways to the waiter. Vincent Gale hid a smile; he was beginning to like the manager. Not that he had a chance—there'd be a bottle upstairs and Heldon would punish it. Gale looked at his watch. It was half past nine and the opening was tomorrow night. Twenty-four hours to sober up, a day to dry out in.

With luck, that is—with very great luck. Vincent Gale drank his coffee thoughtfully. Madame was playing cat with him and only a surprisingly agreeable security officer had saved him from a boredom which he didn't like to think about. Just the same, he'd done well to come. Heldon was past talking to, and if he took a few drinks tomorrow. . . .

If he took a few drinks tomorrow the Prime Minister

would be delighted that his Foreign Secretary had happened to be visiting the shaikhdom. By apparent coincidence, naturally.

Successful administration was the use of coincidence wisely.

Ernest was living on borrowed time and knew it. The Council was to be opened in a day or two, a British junior Minister was arriving for the ceremony, and with these formal if futile ceremonies overhanging him the shaikh wouldn't risk a scandal. But once the visitors departed Ernest couldn't expect to last long. He knew he could not, for he had spotted the beggar who was watching his mistress's house. He'd be a body in the harbour or another desert skeleton. He hoped they'd decently kill him first for vultures he had a horror of.

He wasn't afraid but he was stretched to snapping mentally. A psychiatrist would have explained his strain in his own persuasive patter: stimuli had been applied to him and certain events had followed. Reflexes had resulted. Now the stimuli kept on coming in but the events were entirely different. The strongest nervous systems cracked, indeed the more powerful the conditioning the more severe the breakdown when stimulus and result diverged. And in the remorselessly thorough training which Ernst had been subjected to the most powerful single stimulus had been doctrine. Here was this shaikhdom, its people poor but its income enormous, shamelessly exploited by a hereditary shaikh. Even work in the Terminal went to foreigners with skills. It was a classic revolutionary situation, *ergo* revolution must follow. A catalyst might be needed, a trained revolutionary, but it was heresy beyond damning if he thought of himself as in any way determining what historically was ineluctable. He was agent not cause. Revolution was inevitable, revolution would therefore come.

And it hadn't; it showed in fact tormentingly few signs of even approaching. Ernest had made converts, one in particular he almost trusted, but though the inhabitants of the shaikhdom showed a sullen resentment which entirely followed doctrine they had an equal irresponsibility which most certainly did not. They might riot on some irrelevance, a woman insulted or a mosque supposedly defiled, whereupon they would be easily suppressed by armed Sikhs in formed bodies. But the opening of the Council had seemed to Ernest the perfect opportunity for really effective action. Of course there'd be police on duty but they'd be spread extremely thin, and a handful of determined men had a chance of seizing a gun or two. . . . Grab a police lorry; fire the rest; then a dash for the barracks and armoury. There'd be a picket no doubt, but with the police on the streets it couldn't be a big one. Shoot it out, loot the armoury. Pass out the weapons. Arms in the hands of a willing people and a couple of hundred disorganized Sikhs would be mercenaries to massacre.

It was straight from the book but the book wasn't coast-Arabic: the more Ernest thought of it the less he felt sure. He didn't expect success on a platter, but twenty men might do it provided they were determined ones. It was the proviso which depressed him. He felt for Shaikh Ali's subjects a pity which wrung him physically; they were miserable, they were exploited, they had nothing to lose but their chains. They also had a considerable respect for their private skins; they were ripe for revolution but they weren't the stuff of martyrs. Some shooting would be inevitable and . . .

And they'd given him promises, extravagant oaths of loyalty. Ernest didn't credit them. What should be revolution, arms eagerly taken as the leaders seized the armoury, could collapse in an Arab whimper. If the leaders did seize the armoury. Twenty good men he needed and he had one he almost trusted. The evening could end in nothing more serious than an ignominious demonstration, the febrile noise an Eastern crowd made in anger, perhaps some futile stone-throwing. That wouldn't bring down a house of cards, far less an oil shaikh backed by a British government. It was maddeningly below his hopes; it wasn't what they'd promised him nor conditioned him to look for.

It had never even occurred to Ernest that the laws he had been fed on weren't perhaps laws at all. Instead he blamed himself. Somewhere he'd missed the party line so naturally he'd met failure.

To Ernest on the verge of a mental breakdown the news that Vincent Gale was visiting the shaikhdom came with the simple clarity of Grace. He had tried to kill him in England, but that had been on principle, a matter of producing a theoretical advantage in a set of future circumstances themselves theoretical. But this was unquestioned fact. The murder of a British Foreign Secretary in a shaikhdom already near flash-point would produce immediate and immediately calculable results. They'd call in troops, there'd be howls from the Arab world, America wouldn't like it though the oil was mostly hers. . . .

Anarchy. Ernest could use anarchy for he'd been thoroughly trained to do so. There were a dozen possibilities —envious Arab neighbours, invasion and famine, arson at the Terminal. All led to chaos, to the final collapse of government. He needn't rely on these disappointing natives: instead he could act himself. This fitted so this was truth.

Ernest's tortured mind was suddenly at peace again. A religious man would have thanked his God quietly but Ernest didn't have one. But he slipped from the house, grinning at the beggar as he followed him, tossing him a coin. He went to a silversmith's, buying a bracelet. Then he gave it to his mistress. She stared at him speechless. Money apart, it was the first gift he'd given her.

Vincent Gale looked at his watch as the knock at his door woke him. It was three o'clock precisely. He had a pistol under his pillow but had never fired one in his life. Robert Mortimer had offered it and Gale had accepted. He doubted his ability to damage anyone but himself and had almost declined politely, but it had occurred to him that if by some chance there was trouble and he was found unarmed Mortimer could be facing some rather tiresome questions. So he'd smiled and accepted the pistol. Vincent Gale had the reputation of a certain lack of sympathy but men and women he respected did not share it.

Now he pulled out the pistol, pushing off the safety catch as Mortimer had shown him. He would have confessed to a tiny thrill. Then he swung himself off the bed and, holding the gun still, threw the door open. The thought struck him as he did so that this was probably hopeless technique. Well, he'd very soon know if it was.

George Heldon stood before him. Far from sobering he'd been punishing a private bottle; he said with the portentous solemnity of the soak: 'Your room was next door. I wanted to discuss with you——'

'Good God, we can't talk now.'

'We must. My speech tomorrow. . . .'

Gale stared at him, silent. He could have said things about tomorrow's speech, comment hurtful and destructive. But it was pointless to wound. Heldon had sat down weakly on bed. 'My speech,' he said again.

'You'll be all right on the night.'

'They always say that.'

Gale watched the sad wreck carefully. It was upright still but only just. It was going to pass out. . . .

It did. Deliberately and not without a drunk's strange dignity Heldon rolled over finally.

Gale considered him impassively. Drink had coarsened the thick body to a brutish fat: Heldon was far too gross to carry, and to call for help would promptly raise a scandal. Vincent Gale shrugged—so they'd have to change rooms discreetly. George Heldon was coatless and Gale pulled his trousers off. He left him in shirt and underpants, noticing with a sharp distaste that neither was quite immaculate; he found the key of Heldon's room with the change in a trousers pocket; he took it and his own key too, slipping bare-footed into the corridor. Then he locked Heldon in. It seemed prudent in the circumstances, and it was very unlikely he would wake before Gale himself did.

At the dark ends of the long corridor the Sikh sentries were changing. They were intent on the niceties of what was evidently a drill, moving like automata, guardsmen depressingly *manqués*. A shot would no doubt have alerted them but not a quiet change of rooms. They stared grimly to their formal fronts, smart, soldierly and unseeing. Gale was certain they hadn't noticed him.

He moved softly to Heldon's room next door. It smelt stalely of whisky despite the air conditioning, and for a moment Gale hesitated. Then he shrugged again and took the bed.

In five minutes he was asleep again.

Ernest's plan had been a mixture of the simplicity which he had been taught made a good one and a reliance on blind chance which he was powerless to avoid. The chance was that the night porter at the hotel couldn't read English and wouldn't, moreover, be particularly intelligent. But Ernest had good reason to be hopeful. His major convert, the one he almost trusted, worked in the hotel, and Ernest had had a word with him. . . . Yes, the manager was a Christian Lebanese and there were two excellent hall porters who took turn and turn about by day. They spoke English and French and Arabic but went off at ten sharp. The night clerks were really janitors. . . . Could they read English? It was doubtful if they could read at all. If there was a night plane with a passenger booked for the hotel one of the day porters would meet it. . . . Were the night clerks, then, intelligent? But what would you expect for four shillings a night, no tips and a cup of coffee? And that was considered good.

Still, it was a risk, something where bluff could work or fail, but the first part of the evening would have a reassuring simplicity. Ernst must reach the hotel alive and he knew that his mistress's house was watched. The watcher mightn't kill him out of hand but certainly he'd be followed, and once it was clear he was heading for the hotel the shadow would swell to several. Then he'd be stopped at least. So he must leave unseen but that was easy. He put on his only decent suit, then on top of it a native woman's gown, the long skirt trailing, hiding his shoes. Over his head went the heavy veil. He watched till a woman came in to the house, then he himself slipped out of it. It was a very expert eye which could tell one burq'a-ed woman from another, and even if the shadow were suspicious he wouldn't dare molest him since he risked a knife in his ribs if he happened to be wrong. As it broke he wasn't interested. A woman had entered a house alone and a woman had come out again. Ernest went to the home of the man he almost trusted. There he waited.

At three-fifteen he was in the garden of the hotel, shedding the native clothes. He went to the hotel's front door. It was open and he walked boldly in. The night clerk was snoring across his desk and Ernest woke him roughly; he said with authority but in an Englishman's Arabic: 'I'm a Queen's Messenger. I have a most immediate dispatch for the British Foreign Secretary.'

The clerk looked at him sleepily. He didn't know it, but in his old-fashioned suit Ernest could have passed as a Queen's Messenger among Queen's Messengers. He was the retired Lieutenant-Colonel with the authoritative manner eking out his pension as a sort of superior errand boy. The clerk knew none of this but he recognized the authority. 'Have you documents of identity?'

'Of course.'

Ernest laid on the desk a four-page paper. It was sealed, bound with red ribbon, and carried poundage of one pound sterling. It was a very important-looking document and Ernest had stolen it, almost absent-mindedly, from his land-lady at Derby, a lady who claimed matrimony but had

71

never produced a husband. It had looked so impressive—one never knew. The night clerk opened the document:

WHEREAS unhappy differences have arisen between the Spouses by reason whereof they have agreed to live apart from each other and the Husband has agreed to pay such allowance to the Wife as hereinafter appears . . .

The clerk nodded wisely, handing back the Deed. 'Please come with me, sir.'

They went upstairs one floor. Ernest saw there was a Sikh at each end of the corridor. The clerk spoke to the nearer who seemed to be protesting. . . . Well, so far he's bluffed it. Ernest said in English: 'I'm a Foreign Office courier.' He waved his Separation Deed to show the extravagant seal.

The Sikh banged his boots in a parade ground salute.

At the door of Gale's room the night clerk knocked. . . . No answer. He knocked again. Ernest said impatiently, but keeping his voice quite steady: 'My dispatches won't wait. Haven't you a pass-key?'

'Yes.'

'Then use it.'

For a moment the night clerk hesitated, then he opened the door. Ernest went in quickly, shutting the door behind him. There was a moon outside but the curtains were drawn, and for a moment he waited, accustoming his eyes to the quarter-light. There was a man on the bed, his back to Ernest, sleeping without a sheet. Ernest drew his knife. He laid it, very delicately, on the spot they had shown him, checking, shifting it half an inch. He'd been meticulously instructed. Then all his weight went smoothly against the hilt. There was the suspicion of a sigh. No more.

Ernest eased back a curtain, opening the double windows silently. The drop wasn't dangerous for a man who knew how to fall.

He picked himself up and went back to his friend.

Chapter Eight

It had been Ernest's conviction that the killing of a British
Foreign Secretary in a shaikhdom already dangerously
inflammable must produce a situation where a conflagration
was inevitable. The conclusion would have been reasonable,
even from premises which weren't rigorously Marxist, and
it wasn't events which proved it wrong but the accident
that the Minister of State had been murdered and his senior
left alive. If Gale had died Heldon would hardly have stood
up to the Resident when he arrived that afternoon, for Sir
Walter Woodard, though not intelligent, was a very senior
official and one who saw things in the simple blacks and
whites of his education and age. He would have recommended the immediate dispatch of troops to hold the shaikhdom against the organized subversion which this murder
must presage, and in terms of the purely local situation he
would have had a sensible case for doing so. What he would
have seen less clearly was that the situation wasn't local and
limited. Troops couldn't be sent unless Ali asked for them,
and though he could almost certainly be persuaded or coerced,
soldiers once landed were a great deal more embarrassing
to withdraw. Moreover in the number available immediately
they would be little more than a provocation to the envious

neighbours whom Ernest had considered too, a temptation to invade and grab both quickly and once for all. And there were the glass and steel hot air house in New York, the organized blocks which deplorably held it impotent. Both had to be thought about though perhaps not too seriously. What was important was as usual the realities: the dispatch of troops, ten men or ten thousand, would open a commitment whose end would be quite unseen.

Nevertheless Sir Walter might have prevailed over a Minister of State who was no longer young or in steady health. There could have been an ill-considered telegram back to London and with it at least the chance of the upheaval Ernest had been hoping for, but with Heldon dead and Gale alive the situation had reversed itself. Of two British Ministers one had died but by far the more powerful, by far the cooler-headed, had survived, and instead of Sir Walter's wah-blah-wuffle Vincent Gale had the advantage of the best advice available. It was, as it happened, the Princess Nahid's, for she had summoned him immediately.

He had gone at once though he'd had plenty to do already. He had been woken by Mortimer, shaken for once from his professional calm, and an exchange of terse sentences had briefed them on Heldon's murder. Bolton had joined them and Mortimer had introduced him. Gale gave the instructions immediately necessary. The Resident was arriving by sea at five o'clock (he had an official yacht to visit his Agents and was known to attach importance to his entrances) and meanwhile he was to be informed by radio of Heldon's death. Death? the two policemen asked. Yes, death was enough for the moment. The Foreign Secretary had permitted himself the comment that there was no point in alarming senior officials unnecessarily; he would meet Sir Walter on arrival, and by five o'clock the story might be clearer. A telegram was to be sent to London—the Agent would see to that—and the Air Force was to send an aircraft from its nearest station to fly Heldon's body back.

74

The orders flowed smoothly but Gale knew they were superficial; they disposed of immediate duties but they decided precisely nothing. And there was plenty to be decided. He had started to think seriously when there was a knock at the door. Mortimer went to it, returning with an envelope. He gave it to Vincent Gale.

'You'll excuse me?'

'Of course.'

Gale opened the letter. It was in Madame's own hand. She had heard certain news and would be grateful if Mr. Gale could call on her at his earliest convenience. He said to Geoffrey Bolton: 'The princess would like to see me—should I go?'

'She's a very shrewd woman, I'd go like a shot. I'll come with you if I may, though.'

'She'll want to talk alone, I think.'

'I'll be happy to wait outside, sir.' Bolton's smile was reminiscent. 'There's a very odd collection in that palace of Madame's but I doubt she includes assassins. It's the journey there I'm concerned about.'

'Very well. . . . Is there anything more I should do before we go?'

'The Agent wanted a word with you.'

'Is there something he knows you don't?' Gale had heard about the Agent and didn't rate him highly.

'I shouldn't think so—no, sir.'

'Please make him my excuses then, but ask him if he'll lunch with me.' Gale had spoken to Mortimer but turned back to Bolton. 'Then I'm at your disposal.'

There were a car and two jeeps today, the car in the middle. Bolton himself was driving with a Sikh beside him, another behind with Gale again. This time they had machine pistols in their laps and an air which Gale couldn't quite place. It would have been unfair to call it trigger-happy but if there was shooting the Sikhs would shoot happily. There was a difference but not a great one.

They drove up the central avenue, swinging left sharply just short of the square, and at once they were in the Arab town. The Sikhs fingered their pistols as the leading jeep nudged a passage. For a second it would win it, then the monstrous human tide would flow again. There were donkeys and street stalls in what was at best a lane, an occasional panniered camel blocking it. The sky was a slit which the stifling stale air rose to: where it came in God knew. The smell of native cooking fought with the stink of excrement. Bolton said grimly, not turning his head: 'The avenue is one thing, this another, but it's the only way out to Madame's.'

'Why don't they cut a road to it?'

'Because they don't dare—not another.'

Gale said unexpectedly: 'Tell me, do you like this job?'

'I wouldn't say like. It's—it's a challenge. Look behind you.'

Vincent Gale did so. In the following jeep three Sikhs were kneeling. They had rifles and were covering the flat roofs. Gale asked almost humbly: 'And that's really necessary? For me?'

'Not only for you, sir—for myself, for my men. At least it discourages throwing things. Not bullets perhaps, but a whole lot dirtier. We're not exactly popular.'

'Do you always travel like this?'

'When I come to the bazaar at all. That's when I have to, which I try to keep seldom.'

Vincent Gale didn't answer. He had never liked Sikhs but he'd begun to think well of Bolton.

Without warning the houses thinned into a final despair of shacks and tents, a fringe of slum to what had itself been the worst slum Gale had seen. They drove through a crumbled wall into what seemed to be a sort of park. If, Gale considered, the word wasn't simply a sneer. There were a palm tree or two and ragged children playing. They stared for an instant, then rushed the car savagely, crying for alms.

76

A Sikh raised his rifle butt and Bolton cursed him briefly, apologizing to Vincent Gale. 'They've had this before, you see. It's unavoidable but it still isn't pleasant.' They drove on across the barren earth, bumping in parallel ruts which fitted the jeeps but not the car. The children clung to the car like flies, the flies crawled obscenely round the children's broken eyes. The dust rose chokingly. As it thinned for an instant Gale could see cracked watercourses, an occasional patch of darker ground which might once have been a flower bed. Bolton pointed ahead. 'That's it,' he said.

'That's what?' Gale could see nothing.

'Madame's house. It was Ali's father's before he built that abortion in the square. Then he gave it to his daughter. This used to be the private park and that wall we came through was eight feet high. It's funny in a way, I think.'

Gale said through his handkerchief: 'You've an active sense of humour.'

'Not active—I'd call it serviceable. You know, I've never been to an Arab country which a proper Arab would acknowledge, so I'm not going to generalize about Arabs. All I know is the people here and they've a genius for neglecting things. I went to India once—on leave, to shoot. They're just as feckless and much worse shams but I don't think they really enjoy decay. These people seem to hug it.'

They had stopped, still in convoy, and the dust had begun to settle. Gale could make out a high mud wall topped with what seemed to be battlements in a pattern first cousin to a Ghibelline *merlatura*, and as the dust cloud came lower there was a pair of tall doors. They were wooden, bound with some metal Gale didn't recognize, the arch which carried them framed in surprisingly delicate brickwork. Both men got down and Bolton pulled a bell chain. The bell was inaudible and they both stood waiting.

They waited some time before one door opened slowly. Holding it was the fattest man Gale had ever seen; he was panting as though he had run a mile and his voice, through his gasps, was an agitated alto. He was wearing a long curved sword and clearly he wasn't used to it. A man of normal size and voice took the door away from him. The major-domo struggled with the scimitar and Vincent Gale, incredulous, saw he was trying to draw it. Ceremonially, he hoped; he said politely: '*Ne vous derangez pas.*'

'*Merci, mon excellence.*'

Bolton saluted and turned on his heel. He was too well disciplined to laugh in Gale's presence but as the door shut behind him he leant against a jeep. . . . The Foreign Secretary was committed to an interesting experience. Bolton had been in that house just once. He wasn't, as he'd told Mortimer, on Madame's list, and that had been strictly true. But she'd invited him once and he'd been inside. He lit a cigarette, walking away from the Sikhs to smoke it. Geoffrey Bolton began to laugh. She was a woman, that one, and something more. He made himself a modest bet: Gale wouldn't be talkative driving home.

The smaller man shut the door behind the three of them, shooting formidable bolts and re-hanging a fine iron chain. It had been made by a Christian slave three centuries before. They were standing in a sort of hall rising to the full height of the building, surprisingly cool. It was broken into a central passageway, defined by pillars and fretted arches, and beyond each file of pillars there was an equal space enclosed by beautiful brick walls again. There were doors in these walls but all but one were padlocked. It was severe but not oppressive, for at the end of the central passageway was light, the sense of what could only be a courtyard. They stood for a moment while the major-domo caught his breath back. Then he clapped his hands. He did it across his face since anywhere else he could hardly have made them meet. Three women appeared from the open door, all veiled. The major-domo spoke to them and they formed a procession, the major-domo in front, one woman on either side of Gale, the third behind. The major-domo looked round, then started to waddle forward, his sword-scabbard clanking. They walked towards the courtyard, under another arch and out into a cloister.

Vincent Gale stopped instinctively. This was an Arab house—the rigidly geometrical ornament, the total suppression of human or animal form both emphasized it unmistakably. But that apart it might have been the *cortile* of some convent in Europe's south. The same strong sun, tamed by the slope of the cloister's penthouse, shone into the rectangle they framed. There was a wellhead and even a dovecote, its tenants languid, one wing clipped. Gale walked across the cloister, looking out into the courtyard. There was a storey above it on three sides of the square, the windows shuttered. The fourth side which faced him was one storey higher and its wall towards the cloister was windowless and blank. Gale nodded in recognition: those would be the stables and every sort of store room, and of course they'd face decently outwards. For a moment he felt nostalgia and knew it for what it was; he was sick for the southern sea and not ashamed.

The major-domo touched his arm and they all turned left, then right again. There was a curtain half-way down what he guessed was the west side of the cloister. The brickwork had changed to herringbone and they were walking on a Caucasian runner which Gale, who loved rugs, would have preferred not to tread on. At the curtain they stopped and the major-domo stood aside. One of the women said in English: 'Enter, please sir. The second door.'

Vincent Gale walked into a room whose furniture surprised him. But its occupant surprised him more. The major-domo and burq'a-ed women, the whole house had prepared him for Princess Nahid. What he saw was Madame in a room filled with very French furniture. She wore a short black jacket and bright red slacks, and her feet were bare on superlative rugs. Her toenails matched the trousers and her ample

79

hair—he remembered it loose with a sudden sting—was piled almost carelessly. She was busy with coffee and turned as he came in. As he took her hand and kissed it she said easily: 'I'm glad I've taught you something you didn't know.'

'I'd call that the understatement of the year.'

'Yes?' She passed him a cup of coffee. 'If you were expecting the local brew, I loathe it. It's all sugar and dregs and it constipates me horribly. I hate being constipated.' She nodded across the room at a coffee mill and an old-fashioned jug. 'I make my own, you can drink it safely. And I hope that business turned out all right.'

For a moment he didn't read her, for she had the alarmingly un-English habit of picking up a conversation at the point it had been broken. Then he realized she was talking about their interrupted dinner. 'You mean my tactless private secretary? He was doing his duty, damn him.'

'I knew you were too,' She spoke without malice but also without reprieve. It was something that had happened, it was gone. She said in her easy friendly voice: 'But you've been here some days.'

'I arrived Friday evening.'

'I'd hoped you'd call before.'

'They advised me to wait till you sent for me.'

'I know they did—I made sure they would.'

'I see,' he said. He didn't.

'I wanted to see what you'd do, you see. A feminine little thing perhaps, but then I'm a woman.' She was suddenly serious. 'But we've things more important to talk about. Somebody tried to kill you.'

'You've heard I changed rooms then?' She nodded and he went on. 'And it begins to look as though there was another attempt on me in England. I had an accident in my car and a man called Charles Russell . . .'

'I've met him, he's a charmer.'

'. . . told me he thought the steering had been tampered with. I didn't pay much attention, but when I got down here there was one of his men as bodyguard. Then if I hadn't changed rooms with Heldon I'd have a knife in my back this moment.'

'Are you frightened?' she asked casually.

'Of course.'

'I'm glad.'

He said with a hint of anger: 'I'd have guessed you'd prefer a hero.'

'I know you would, Vincent. You know how to please a woman but you're sometimes a little innocent about them. Perhaps if you'd liked one well enough to risk marrying her. . . .' She was watching his expression change. It had been relaxed, even eager, but now it was detached again, a disciplined face, a lawyer's. She went on on a note of mischief. 'What I like in a man is guts and men who admit they're frightened mostly have them.'

'Could I have some more coffee, please.'

She laughed as she rose. 'You must be marvellous at Question Time.' She gave him the coffee and waited for him to drink it. 'And what do we do now?' she asked.

'I think we open the Council as arranged. Tonight—there's no point in postponement. I'm here so I'll do it. The dinner before must go, of course. We can't have a dinner with Heldon dead.'

She nodded at once. 'I think that's right. The Resident is arriving at five o'clock and I'm very glad you're here. He's spent ten years on this coast, he knows us all too well, but he's a man with limitations. Left to handle this alone he could easily act irrevocably. So we'll open the Council and then we'll consider. It loses us nothing and it gains us a day to think in.'

'It's a pity you're not the shaikh,' he said.

'That's not really a compliment but I've heard it before.' Her mood changed unexpectedly into an intimacy as rare as it was rewarding. 'Once when I was a little girl. . . .' She broke off suddenly. 'I hope I'm not boring you.'

'Never.'

'Our blood's running pretty thin, you know. Ali's childless and rather weak; he's neither fish nor fowl nor good red commie. I think my father knew it. I was his favourite and I adored him. So once when I was little. . . .' She stopped again, playing with her cup. 'Ali had made some childish boob, fallen off a horse, I think, and my father lost his temper. We were all three together and my father put his hand on my head. He was still in a rage but now he wasn't shouting. He was always at his worst like that. "This should have been my son," he said. I've never forgotten it. Nor, I'm afraid, has Ali.'

Vincent Gale didn't answer; he had nothing to say. As the Princess Nahid got up he asked: 'Will you be at the opening?'

'No, I shall not.'

'Are you frightened?' He had spoken on an impulse, half in a retaliation which he knew to be petty. But she answered without anger.

'It doesn't arise. In this room I am one thing but outside another. Women don't attend state functions.'

'It would have been pleasanter for your presence.'

'Muffled up like a mummy?' She laughed again. 'If that was another compliment it's more delicate than you intended.' She held out her hand. 'Come and see me before you go. 'Don't wait for me to send for you.' She was mocking him and he knew it. 'Just come.'

'I will.'

Gale walked back through the curtain and the procession re-formed. The great door swung open and closed again behind him. For a moment the light blinded him, then he saw Bolton waiting. He climbed into the car with what might almost have been a sigh.

They drove back to the hotel in total silence.

Bolton and Robert Mortimer had dutifully accepted that the Council should be opened as planned, though both would have preferred that it should not. But they could recognize necessity. The evening plane was bringing in such journalists as the Foreign Office had been able to interest in what the Press as a whole suspected was a self-evident political sham, and if the opening were hole-and-corner too the whole thing would stink to heaven. Not that it didn't already. The journalists would be interested in Heldon's death too, and the story for that was the simple and brutal truth: Heldon had been murdered but the murderer hadn't been found yet. The Press might smell politics but for the moment they hadn't a lead. Rich-looking foreigners were murdered in shaikhdoms for reasons quite other than politics. But cancel the opening and they'd have something more to go on. And how they'd go.

So Bolton and Mortimer had accepted the public opening, though their professional difficulties had now been considerably increased. The original plan had been for dinner in the palace, the populace in the square outside. The police band would play and there would be fireworks and junketings. Then the shaikh and the bigwigs would have processed across the square—they would, that is, if a way could have been kept open for them—and so into the Council House. It wasn't big so there couldn't have been a crowd inside. Heldon would do his formal stuff, then the usual boring speeches, and finally Shaikh Ali, with the Resident for good measure, would have appeared on the balcony. The loyal rabble would cheer like mad . . .

One had hoped so.

But now that was clearly out. There couldn't be a banquet with Heldon just murdered, and having Gale walk across the square would obviously be tempting providence. So they'd start straight in the Council House and there was a back entry into it. To that extent it was easier now, but there'd still be a crowd in the square unless Bolton were allowed to clear it, and given the limitation that the opening must be public that was the one thing he couldn't do. And Ernest could be among that crowd.

Robert Mortimer had been worried, for the orthodox course with a killer was to arrest him and hold him safely. But he'd seen Bolton's difficulty. Bolton couldn't comb the bazaar for Ernest since on this of all evenings he daren't risk trouble. This evening Ernest had him fixed.

And Bolton had other worries too. He'd been reasonably confident about Gale's personal safety but he was also inescapably responsible for good order in the square. And with Ernest still operating he couldn't underwrite it, even if he could have pulled him in in time. For Ernest would have friends and Bolton didn't know all of them. One or two he might guess but one or two wasn't good enough. The crowd outside would cheer like crazy. . . .

Or maybe they wouldn't.

It had been left at the thorough precautions which they could take for the awkward evening, but the future had been considered too. Mortimer had said firmly: 'We can't leave a killer at large indefinitely.'

'Of course we can't.' Bolton lit a cheroot, blowing a smoke ring on the stagnant air. 'I can't drag-net the bazaar but if I knew where he was I could make a quick grab for him.' Bolton was silent. 'I mean to,' he said finally. 'We must. But tomorrow.'

'And his friends? His organization?'

'Will quietly fall to pieces. I know my locals.'

'If I could help. . . .'

'I think you could. It's Stavridis I'm going for first. He may not know now where Ernest is hiding but he could probably find out. If he tried to, that is—if I made him. And I've plenty on Stavridis as you know.'

'And where do I come into that?'

'You sit in on the interview. You're Major Robert Mortimer of the Security Executive, and with your permission I'll introduce you as just that.' Bolton smiled his amiably sardonic smile. 'It will help,' he said dryly.

'So we're back at this evening.'

'When I can offer no guarantee. All I can do is to have every policeman available in or around that square.' Geoffrey Bolton reflected again. 'I emphasize around,' he said.

'I wasn't asking.'

'Thanks for the vote of confidence. I wish I could second it, but the evening could turn out badly, that's a fact.'

'If I may ask—how badly?'

Bolton said dourly: 'You'll know if it happens.'

The stout man was in one of his famous rages. The room had been a prince's once and there was plenty of room for rages. He was pacing it furiously, swearing in the name of a God he officially didn't believe in. 'The fools,' he said, 'the bloody fools.'

'I admit it's an outrage. Trying to kill the British Foreign Secretary in England, killing a Minister of State in that ridiculous shaikhdom——'

'An outrage!' The stout man bounded across the room, astonishingly agile for his weight. He faced the lean man, and for a moment the general flinched. But no blow fell. Instead the stout man waved a plump but still muscular fist. 'An outrage, indeed! Can't you see it's a *danger*?' The stout man began to swear again. 'Oriental barbarians. Cretinous clowns.' He choked; recovered himself. Almost calmly he said: 'They'll have us at war yet.'

Chapter Nine

At five minutes to five Vincent Gale was on the Promenade waiting for the Resident's yacht to tie up to the single pier. He watched the approach with interest, for he had recently declined to spend money on replacing her. She wasn't really a yacht but a medium cabin cruiser quite incapable of sea-going, but she could creep up the coast and the Resident drew prestige from her. But not, it seemed, sufficient. He had suggested a newer model and the Foreign Secretary had refused to pay for it. This one had ten years' life in her and that, Gale guessed, was plenty. In five years' time, or ten perhaps, there wouldn't be a Resident.

A gangway went down and for a moment nothing happened. Then His Excellency appeared on deck and at once there was activity. Two sailors blew boatswain's pipes (the complement was three) but were immediately drowned by the police band ashore. They crashed into The Queen, in time in a formal way, but mysteriously turning the banal air into the bastard of dirge and requiem. Their European repertoire was exactly three pieces: they could manage the National Anthem, they had a highly personal version of 'The British Grenadiers', and their third was a tune which a very expert ear might vaguely have related to 'The Lincolnshire Poacher'. Now they thumped through The Queen and waited.

The Resident began to move heavily down the gangway. The four men awaited him—Gale, the Agent, Geoffrey Bolton and Mortimer. Bolton and the Agent were in uniform, Mortimer was not, but he was meticulously inspecting the Resident's as he advanced. Uniforms were a hobby of his and he had one of the best collections of coloured prints of them in England. His Excellency was in tropical whites and Mortimer nodded approvingly. That meant that his plumage was a good deal less exuberant than it might otherwise have been, but it also meant that he'd be pleasanter to stand close to. Mortimer checked the details:

HELMET—*White service regulation pattern without chin-strap, bearing on the front a gilt badge, the Royal Arms with supporters. Plain white pugaree.*

Except, Mortimer remembered, that they spelt it *pagri* to show a knowledge of the language. His eyes moved lower.

SWORD—*Of regulation pattern, with black scabbard and gilt mountings. The sword should be worn on paying or returning official visits, and on the other occasions of ceremony. It should be carried in a white frog, projecting through the slit on the left side of the coat, and attached to a belt worn under the latter. On these occasions a spike should be worn on the helmet.*

Mortimer looked up again. Yes, the Resident had a spike on it. If he'd only been wearing corsets which, disastrously, he wasn't, Mortimer would have awarded him Excellent Turn-out. His Excellency landed and gave rather a weak salute. Mortimer dropped him four points at once. The police band was playing 'The Grenadiers' and Mortimer knew it shouldn't be. The Resident shook hands all round, then turned formally to Gale, saying with fat solemnity:

87

'I received your message that Heldon had died. This is inconvenient—very inconvenient indeed.' He added as an afterthought: 'And sad, of course.' The Resident didn't sound sad at all. He was a man of the Right and all others were enemies. He changed gear ponderously. 'But I'm delighted to have you here.' His Excellency did not appear so. The words seemed to be wrung from him.

'I'm delighted to *be* here.'

'Ah yes, of course—the opening. Now that you're here. . . .'

'But I didn't mean that.'

'Then I'm not sure I follow you.'

Gale said urbanely: 'Heldon didn't just die. He was murdered.'

The Resident went turkey red, then appropriately began to gobble. 'Murdered? Did you say murdered?'

'Yes. By accident.'

'But how can you murder by accident?'

'I was less than precise—I'm sorry. What I should say was that the intention to murder was deliberate but that accidentally the wrong man was killed.' Gale smiled his most court-room smile. 'The target,' he said, 'was me.'

'Good God.'

There was a moment of silence and Mortimer listened to it. He knew the Resident's reputation and clearly Gale did too. There was a mischief in Gale's manner but also a long strong patience. After all he was a Minister; he had to work with the diplomatists.

But the Resident was sorting it out. It was two plus two and he made that four; he said triumphantly: 'So somebody tried to kill you?'

'Yes.'

'Here—in my Agency?'

'Yes.'

'And who was this man?'

'A foreign agent.'

There was silence again on the listless air. At last His

Excellency said: 'Then I suggest we go aboard my yacht. We can decide there what to do. The necessary decisions——"

'I don't think there are any, or not for the moment. The dinner has had to come off of course, but the opening stands as arranged. Since I happen to be here I'll take it. Afterwards I hope you'll come to my hotel.'

'But your personal safety——'

'Major Mortimer here is an officer of the Security Executive.' Vincent Gale smiled again, adding with a gesture which you could take as a bow if you wished to: 'An institution for which I have even more respect today than I had a week ago.'

'I don't understand you.'

'I'm not sure you were meant to.' It was a reproof but delivered blandly—too blandly, since the Resident didn't notice it; he ploughed on relentlessly.

'But public disturbances. . . .' His Excellency fingered his collar—stand-up collar with detachable dark blue gorgets of varying pattern according to rank. His Excellency's was a high one. Incredibly he added: 'The Queen's Peace——'

'I have entire confidence in Chief Superintendent Bolton.'

The Resident made a despairing stand. 'But the situation generally——'

'Is intolerably hot in this sun. I see the Agent has brought you a car.' Gale held out his hand. 'I'm looking forward to seeing you this evening.' He walked with the Resident to the Agent's car. It wouldn't start immediately and that ruined an exit. Gale stood patient and silent while the band murdered the Poacher, then walked to the police car with Bolton and Mortimer. Once settled in the back he said: 'Can you get beer here—cold?'

'You can at the hotel.'

'Then I elect myself host. We've earned it.'

The Council chamber wasn't a big one since it wasn't intended for many men. There were a canopied chair for the shaikh and, stretching away from it, a long table with pompous leather-backed seats imported from an expensive English furnisher. It was a narrow room, blind on three sides but with French windows on the fourth giving on to a balcony which overlooked the square. In Europe it would have been much too dark but here it was pleasantly cool. This evening Shaikh Ali was sitting in the chair of state, Gale on his right hand and, to his left, the Resident in full fig again. He was sweating but not insufferably. On Gale's side of the table three men sat stiffly and on the Resident's there were four empty chairs for the elected majority not yet elected. Along one wall stood a double file of spectators and court functionaries, and Gale could see Mortimer amongst them, incongruous in English clothes. But not too incongruous. He was skilful at making himself inconspicuous.

Vincent Gale wasn't at ease. It was one thing to approve a sham, quite another to be faced with it. He looked at the three nominated members, sensing that they weren't quite happy sitting. A fortnight ago they would have been standing with the double row of court retainers. . . . And the elected majority? There was going to be an election, there was an elaborate electoral roll, but it would be shameless self-deception to suppose that they'd be different. One or two electors would probably make a pound or two and the rest would simply be suborned. In King Charles Street one suspected it, suppressing the thought distastefully; here there was no escape.

Shaikh Ali looked round the room; stood up. He was wearing the most formal of his robes and he said in an Arabic which perhaps three men in ten could follow: 'This was to have been a happy occasion but it has been overshadowed by a death which we all regret. This is not a time for speeches.' The shaikh looked at Gale and Gale rose in turn. He handed across a parchment scroll, conscious that the action was both absurd and an indignity. Shaikh Ali's face was expressionless. He took the scroll and said in English: 'I am grateful for Her

Majesty's gift.' His voice wasn't grateful but it was also without irony. It had been exquisitely done.

'I will convey Your Highness's thanks.' Vincent Gale had sat down again but the shaikh stayed standing. After a moment he said with formality: 'We should now show ourselves to the people. You, Mr. Gale, myself and Your Excellency—we should go on to the balcony.' The Resident struggled upright, taking the shaikh's right side. Gale took his left and they walked towards the windows. A servant swung them open, then shut them with ceremony. They stood on the balcony, waiting.

For an instant nothing happened, then the windows behind them disintegrated. They broke in a single appalling crash as the barrage of stones came up at them. The shaikh put a hand to a bloody face and Gale had been hit in the chest. He hadn't been hurt but the Resident had; he was lying behind the parapet, gasping, apparently winded. Shaikh Ali said mildly: 'Deplorable.' Somebody had opened what was left of the doors. The shaikh turned on his heel, extending his hand politely: 'After you, Mr. Gale.' Half a brick caught him solidly at the back of his head-dress and for a second he staggered. He did not fall. 'After you, Mr. Gale,' he said again. His voice hadn't changed. Vincent Gale bent down quickly, grabbing the Resident; he grabbed him by his collar —stand-up, with detachable dark blue gorgets denoting rank—towing him behind him on the seat of his braided trousers. The shaikh, without haste, brought up the rear. The Agent appeared and took the Resident. Shaikh Ali ignored him. He sat down again in the chair of state, looking at Vincent Gale. 'I trust you're not hurt, sir?'

Gale shook his head. 'And Your Highness?'

'Not a scratch.' He had blood on his face but he didn't seem aware of it; he said conversationally: 'An unsettling experience which I won't make worse by apology. What I regret is that I cannot offer you whisky. May I send for some coffee?'

'Coffee would be refreshing, yes.'

Shaikh Ali clapped his hands. The Agent and another man were attending to the Resident. 'My physician,' the shaikh explained. 'Not that I think His Excellency is seriously hurt. Winded, I'd guess.'

'Painful at his age.'

'Yes.' Shaikh Ali began to laugh; he fought it and controlled himself, adding indifferently: 'Well, he was always expendable.' The stone-throwing had stopped, but outside there was the terrifying sound of a crowd in anger. In Europe it would have been a roar of rage: here it was a sort of scream. They seemed to be chanting something in the intervals. Ali was listening, then he suddenly frowned. 'Really,' he said, 'they can't say that.' He took off his spectacles, handing them to Gale. 'Please be so kind.' Then he rose in a single movement, stalking to the window. Somebody tried to stop him but he brushed him aside. Shaikh Ali was on the balcony.

There was the instant silence of utter surprise. Into it Ali shouted; Shaikh Ali went on shouting.

Gale turned to the man beside him. 'What's he saying?' he asked.

'It is very bad words.' It was one of the nominated Councillors and his English was limited.

'You mean he's abusing them?'

'Please?'

'What sort of bad words?'

'Please excuse.'

'But I don't.'

The Councillor dredged his vocabulary. 'It is issue of woman not married to man.' For a moment the Councillor brightened—a word had come back to him. 'Whore,' he said happily.

'He's calling them bastards?'

'I think.'

'They are.'

'Please?'

'Never mind. Go on.'

'Too bad—too rude.'

'Go *on*!'

'It is man going to bed with sister, mother too. It is man making love to camel. It is dogs and pigs and . . .'

Outside there was a single shot.

Ernest and the man he almost trusted had left his house an hour before, joining the crowd which was growing in the square. It was still buzzing with Heldon's death, the sort of news it would have been impossible to conceal even if Bolton had thought the attempt worth while. To Ernest it had been a bitter blow—he'd killed the wrong man and that was hardly professional; worse, he was now back on his original plan, the one which depended on these undependable people. He was dressed as an Arab and falsely though discreetly haired, but he knew there was a chance that he'd be recognized and arrested. If he were, he'd insisted, the operation must go on: this was a group commitment, the loss of one man irrelevant. But he'd known that if they got him that would end it, and even if they didn't success was something which he'd only half believed in. He couldn't raid an armoury single-handed: for that he had to have twenty men with arms in the hands of such as survived. Each of the men who'd sworn to him was to have picked himself a policeman, then, when the stones went up, to have jumped him for his weapon. It must be simultaneous to have a chance. It hadn't been difficult to organize the stone-throwing since nobody risked too much by it, and in the event the demonstration had exceeded Ernest's hopes. The stones went up and . . .

Nothing. Not a man of the twenty moved.

Ernest had cursed but the man he almost trusted blushed. He wasn't a coast Arab but a man from the desert. He was savagely ashamed. What made it worse was that he wasn't surprised; what made it quite intolerable was the suspicion that Ernest himself would be anything but astonished. Ernest was a foreigner and these gutless faithless Arabs. . . .

The stone-throwing had stopped and Ali was on the balcony alone. It had all misfired, it was an ignominy, a personal shame. The man Ernest almost trusted sighed. He was still behind his Sikh. The Sikh had brought his rifle across his chest and he was swearing in Punjabi, uncertain what to do. The desert Arab knifed him neatly. The Sikh folded slowly, dropping the rifle. The Arab bent to pick it up—one man at least could still hold his neck straight.

He died as he straightened it.

Geoffrey Bolton had told Mortimer that he would have men around the square as well as in it, and Harnam Singh was one of them. He was stationed on a roof-top, lying on a blanket, fondling a rifle with a telescopic sight. He was the best shot in Bolton's police force.

He was looking at Havildar Ranjit Singh. He hated him for he'd just been promoted. Harnam Singh was a Mazbi and the havildar was a Jat. Ranjit Singh's family were yeoman landowners, and he had the fine precise features of the Jat Sikh of respectable ancestry. Harnam Singh's were labourers —his nose was coarse, his beard too wiry. But he'd served longer than Ranjit, he was stronger and he could shoot better. He spat in disgust. The promotion had been a typical Jat *banawat*.

Harnam was watching Ranjit as he fell. At first he thought he'd fainted. . . . Good, they'd probably strip him. Fainting on duty wasn't something taken lightly. Harnam Singh looked again. He had a marksman's eyesight and the arc lights in the square were strong. There was something in Ranjit's back, a knife, and on the white of his jacket a dark stain spreading slowly.

For a second Harnam hesitated. His orders had been careful, even minatory: he should shoot to protect, but browning into the crowd could have only one outcome and that would

94

be Harnam's court martial. A man had bent down for the fallen rifle. Harnam Singh put his own up, following the movement down; he'd fire at the bottom or not at all and he'd have to risk a ricochet. The man took the rifle and his head began to rise again. Harnam Singh had it steady on the cross-hairs of his telescope. He took the first pressure and then the second.

Shaikh Ali bin Hasan bin Ibrahim had stopped shouting on the shot. Outside there was the scuffle of running feet, inside the Chamber the silence of shocked uncertainty. The shaikh watched for perhaps ten seconds, then turned his head to the silent room; he beckoned to Vincent Gale. 'But come and look at this,' he said. 'It's interesting.'

Gale walked on to the balcony. The lights were still blazing and for a moment he blinked in them. Then he got his focus. Two Sikhs were putting a third on to a stretcher and a fourth was standing guard over what seemed to be a body on the ground. These five men apart the square was empty.

'But where have they gone?' It sounded foolish and probably was but Gale asked it instinctively.

'They've all run away.'

'And the police?'

'Assisting them to run, no doubt.' His Highness stood motionless then, astonishingly, groaned. 'My people,' he said; he faced Vincent Gale. 'You can have them and welcome.'

Shaikh Ali went back to his palace through a connecting corridor and at once to his bed. He lay down gratefully for he was utterly exhausted. Any sort of scene exhausted him: emotion spent him—his own or other people's. And he knew he was near the end. A greedy man might have soldiered on, or a raging patriot, or simply a man who loved power for its own sake. He was none of these things; he was a man with a patrimony which he was ready to make concessions to retain since he'd learnt as a boy in Switzerland that nowadays that was necessary. There was an extraordinary theory called progressive taxation under which not only did the rich pay more than the poor paid (the young Ali had accepted that as reasonable) but also were taxed at higher rates. Extraordinary. But it seemed to be universally accepted in the incomprehensible Western world. Not that taxation worried him, he was a ruler and didn't pay it, but concessions were demanded just the same.

This Council, for instance—he knew what that meant. He didn't fear its members, he had something on all of them, but the Council itself was a wedge which the English would tap at mercilessly; they'd broaden the crack till he wasn't a shaikh at all. In a calculable time he'd be one of those pathetic maharajahs, a man with a title and no influence on events at all, what had once been a patrimony reduced to a privy purse, a by no means generous allowance from the state which had supplanted him.

Ali stretched on his bed. . . . Just the same it would have been worth a fight if the odds hadn't become impossible. He knew that he wasn't a fighter, not as his father and grandfather would have understood the word, but he wasn't a coward either, and he had all the disinclination of the man of property to losing it when he needn't. He could have held for a year or two—five perhaps—but now it was hardly on. Or not in circumstances which he regarded as worth the effort. A British junior Minister had been murdered in his territory and it was humanly certain that the real target had been the Foreign Secretary himself; there'd been a riot and a shooting at the most formal of functions; that ass of a Resident had been contemptuously stoned. Ali totted it up, looking at the total as he was sure the British would see it. There was only one thing they could really do: in practice they'd take him over. It was true that under the Treaty they couldn't put troops in unless he asked for them, but there were at least three ways, all of them disagreeable, that pressure to do so could be brought on him. His father might have stood up to it but he wasn't his father; he was a man of wealth who wished quietly to enjoy its use. Quietly—that was the essence. Shaikh Ali would never be quiet again. Not if he stayed the shaikh.

He rose from his bed, walking across the room and opening a wall safe. He took out an account book, studying it carefully. . . . Thirty-six million Swiss francs. Putting that in English, which was the last thing he intended to, that was three million pounds.

He could live modestly on that if he were really economical.

Chapter Ten

By noon next day Vincent Gale had made his decisions and
had passed them to those who would carry them out. He
considered that in one thing he'd been lucky, for the Resident
hadn't offered the complication of advice which, though
futile, Gale might at least have had to listen to. Instead Sir
Walter had retreated upon one of the classic expedients
of his profession; he'd gone diplomatically sick. The Foreign
Secretary had been amused by it. . . . Unfortunate Sir
Walter. He'd made his careful entrance in his yacht and had
been told in effect that he wasn't essential; then he'd appeared
on a balcony and promptly he'd been stoned; he'd been hit
in his ample belly and been dragged like a sack to safety. By
his Foreign Secretary at that. It had hardly been impressive,
hardly in the tradition of a senior diplomatist. Putting it
bluntly he'd cut a very poor figure. So there'd been a stiff
little note of stiffer regret. . . . Mr. Gale would understand
that Sir Walter's injury made it necessary that he seek
medical attention at once; he remained, as in duty bound,
his Minister's humble, obedient servant.

His yacht had sailed and Sir Walter with it.

. . . Excellent. And a discussion with Bolton and Mortimer
had been reasonably reassuring. The Agent had had to be

present too, but events had overawed him, and though he was evidently inconsiderable he had the compensating virtue that he seemed to be aware of it. The re-postings now necessary would be easy. Gale himself would return to England and report to the Prime Minister. It was his guess that the Resident's diplomatic indisposition could be diplomatically extended, in which case they'd replace him by somebody who occasionally looked at the year on the calendar. Such men could be found, though not easily in the Foreign Service. And the Agent they'd change for some young up-and-comer. They'd give him more authority and see that he thrived on it.

And Gale had been impressed by Geoffrey Bolton. A killer was at large still, more important a professional trouble-maker, and Bolton had explained both his difficulties and his plan. Gale had thought it sensible. Bolton couldn't, it seemed, risk a hunt in the bazaar, but he could make what in practice would be a limited invasion if he knew, and precisely, just where to invade. He'd been confident that he could obtain his information. Gale hadn't pressed him, for he never pressed officials when once he'd decided to trust them. So this Ernest would be arrested and the law would take its course. Major Mortimer had had ideas on that. Nobody wanted a political scandal, so they'd play that side *pianissimo*. There'd be no need to mention Gale's accident in England —for one thing there wasn't a shred of proof and for another the jurisdiction would be different. Legal complications, if Mortimer might say so, were the devil. So Ernest would be shipped down the Coast and duly stand trial for murder. . . . Of whom? Of the Minister of State by political design or of Mr. Heldon by accident? Mortimer had thought neither. It would be impossible to conceal that Gale had changed rooms with Heldon, but there was a chance that any other aspect could be, well, muffled. It was a pity that Ernest hadn't *stolen* anything. . . . Mortimer had looked at Bolton and Bolton, almost imperceptibly, had nodded. Mr. Vincent

Gale of the Inner Bar had opened his mouth, then shut it again decidedly. He wasn't here as a Queen's Counsel but as Her Majesty's Foreign Secretary. The lady was identical but the duties demanded different.

And Major Mortimer? he had asked—he intended to stay here? Perhaps. Mortimer's formal assignment would end when he had seen the Foreign Secretary safely on to his aircraft that evening, but thereafter he'd seek instructions from his chief. Vincent Gale had nodded. Charles Russell was another official he wholly trusted, and Bolton and Mortimer would be a formidable team.

When the meeting was over Gale poured himself a lager from the refrigerator in the sitting-room. He drank it reflectively, conscious that his mood was rather different from what it should have been. A modest self-congratulation wouldn't have been unseemly but he felt no desire to indulge it. On paper he'd done admirably. There'd been foresight to start with, entirely justified, and the sheer good fortune to follow it which any Minister needed if he intended to survive politically. The Prime Minister would be pleased with him: he wasn't pleased with himself. Maybe he was angrier than he knew—a man had tried to kill him twice. Gale shook his head slowly. His mind was too well-disciplined to accept a rationalization which he knew to be irrational. He stared into his beer. . . . But it was a sense of inadequacy, almost of loss. You sat in King Charles Street pulling the strings and half-way across the world men lived and died. Especially died. Men like this Ernest, a subversionist, a killer. He'd take a man's life on a phrase of doctrine but he'd also risk his own. And one day he'd lose it. But there was something he believed in, something to hold if the grey days came, old age and with luck the whisky. And so in his way had that preposterous Sir Walter, a mistaken sense of a non-existent mission. Absurd, of course—both errors were contemptible to a sophisticated mind. No doubt. But both were fires, fires warmed a man, and Vincent Gale. . . .

He finished his beer and looked at the time. In half an hour he'd be wishing Madame goodbye. He'd come as her guest and he'd leave as her visitor. She'd have seen through the whole arrangement now, and she wasn't a woman to be used with impunity. So she'd receive him and mock him and wish him good fortune; she'd forget him in a fortnight, he'd be gone. Back to his office with his experience and intelligence, a Minister, a splendid thing. . . .

She wouldn't give a bob for that and this morning he didn't either.

He was driven to her house again with precautions even more thorough than those on the first occasion. Previously he had thought them excessive, the over-insurance of conscientious police and security officers, but now he did not. Nevertheless, necessary or otherwise, they did not improve his temper. He would have admitted that his mood was dour. The sense of inadequacy still dogged him, the uneasy realization that first-class administration was something which could look humiliatingly remote when confronted with direct and personal action. It had never pleased him overly that he was Foreign Secretary since he knew that the short list from which he'd been chosen had been a short one of necessity. What was disturbing was the unexpected insight that this splendid resounding office was in a real sense irrelevant. In the pinches, where men risked their lives, an efficient computer would balance the risks as well or better. And that was what he really did—he balanced the risks of other men. That wasn't a reassuring thought. He was Her Majesty's Foreign Secretary but he was also Vincent Gale. A man, or he liked to think so. On his way to see a woman, too.

The great wooden door swung open with its air of discreet reluctance and the fat major-domo was panting in Gale's face again. The same three women appeared from the side door, the same procession formed. They took him to Princess Nahid.

He felt the change in atmosphere at once. Madame was wearing French clothes again but today they were the clothes of a cold correctitude. She wasn't making coffee but clapped for it as he entered. A woman brought it, offering it formally. With an equal formality Madame said: 'It is kind of you to call on me. You must be a busy man today.'

He said, trying to turn it: 'You told me that once before.'

'You've a very good memory.'

. . . Hell, they were going to quarrel. All right, if she wanted it, she'd certainly picked the moment. He'd a temper himself though he'd try to control it. But not, he decided, so hard that it hurt.

'Won't you sit down?' the princess said.

He did so, waiting, watching her sip the coffee. It was the local brew which she'd said she hated and she didn't do more than taste it. Vincent Gale said politely: 'This is excellent coffee.'

'I'm so glad you like it. My brother drinks a lot of it.'

'His Highness. . . . Yes, of course.'

She said without change of face or voice: 'Tell me why you came down here, please. I mean to the shaikhdom at all.'

It was a question he had expected and he'd decided how to answer it; he owed her the truth and he gave it simply. 'If you feel you've been used that's partly true, but I hope you'll believe only partly. I'd been given no warning of what happened last night. What I was afraid of was that Heldon would make a fool of himself—he drank too much and talked dangerous nonsense. I couldn't come officially, I couldn't supersede him, but I wanted to be present as a sort of reinforcement. That means that I could only come unofficially, and I could only come unofficially if somebody invited me. So I fished for an invitation from you.'

He watched her as she considered it. He hadn't smiled as he'd spoken. Disarming smiles he disliked himself and Madame would despise them. She said at length: 'That isn't an answer to give a woman.'

'It's an answer to a princess, perhaps. Shaikh Ali's sister.'

'You needn't doubt I believe you. And I've always wanted to see a British Minister in action.'

'Whom you once said you didn't like much.'

'Whom I once said I didn't like at all, but now I'll accept the much.' She looked at him steadily, for an instant less hostile. 'You behaved very well last night.'

'I hadn't time to think,' he said. 'Your brother was magnificent.'

'But you're going to break him, aren't you? You're going to strip him of what he values. This ridiculous Council is only a step to it.'

'If you're talking about power politics I don't think he values power.'

'I'm not and he doesn't. What he values is peace and quiet, and that he'll never have again.'

He didn't reply and she rose to her feet; he rose with her as she faced him. She had been calm before, correct and distant, now she was suddenly angry. Her soft voice slid brutally into the shrill scold of the oriental. 'You don't do much for us, do you? You use the oil but you duck your responsibilities.'

'Colonialism isn't popular nowadays.'

'Colonialism! Who cares about words.' She had controlled her voice but not her rage. 'What do you give us for what you take? You appoint a donkey as a Resident and a stooge as his local Agent. My brother just wants to be left alone but that doesn't suit you either. So you lumber him with this Council. Does *that* salve your consciences? It looks democratic but what will it do for us? And I don't mean for me—for *us*. You've driven twice to this house and there's only one way to it. You'll know what I mean if you're not quite blind.'

'Then you'd like to be taken over?' He had intended an irony but achieved an explosion. For a second he thought she'd strike him.

'I don't care a curse who takes us over—it won't be you

103

in any case. You're finished, you're second-rate. What I despise is this hiding behind the legal forms. We're an independent Arab state—like hell we are! Would you bother to keep a police force here if the oil didn't come across us?' She fought herself, for an instant cooled; she said almost reasonably: 'I imagine you think I'm an oil-bitch myself but if so I'm a very small one. Ali makes me an allowance, two per cent of what they pay him on the throughput of the Terminal. A half of that keeps me comfortably and half I give away. But ninety-eight per cent is wasted.' She turned to him in a sudden appeal. 'Don't you think that you owe us the decencies? At least to spread the money while you're here with us at all.'

'We can hardly run the flag up—not today.' He was trying again to turn her. It didn't work.

'It simply isn't good enough.' She was more angry than ever. 'It's having it both ways, it isn't fair.'

'It's a pity you're not the shaikh,' he said. He had said it before but he meant it now.

'Of course it's a pity I'm not the shaikh! Have you any idea what it's like to be a woman in the Arab world? A suspect woman half foreign in blood and more than half foreign in everything else. And with a brother whom I love, poor wet.'

'I can see it must be difficult.'

'You bloody English! Your stupid understatements! You're flying away this evening. *Bad luck to you*. A man would stay and see it out.'

It was utterly unexpected and it caught him flat-footed. 'But I can't possibly stay as a sort of unauthorized adviser. In any case there's the Cabinet——'

Madame said something unfriendly about the Cabinet.

'But I'll do everything possible.' He was trying to be sensible, realizing too late that it was the worst line of all. She lost control finally. 'Get out,' she said. 'Away from me.'

'It's a poor way to go.'

'Of course it is—you're a very poor thing. You know what I think?' He told her, with some indifference, that no, he did not. 'I think that man Ernest is twice the man you are. Not because he's a killer—any fool can kill a man—but because he's got something alive inside, a faith if you must have the word. You haven't got that and you're no better than my brother. Just a whole lot more powerful and that makes it worse.'

'Good-bye,' he said.

She turned away and Gale turned too. The great door opened and shut again and that, he thought, was that. He wasn't angry or even hurt.

The reaction, he knew, came later.

Vincent Gale had been allowing himself a rare moment of depression but Stavridis had solid and pressing reasons to be thoughtful. It hadn't been his morning. He was one of the very few who had made money from the oil which flowed across the shaikhdom, and he lived in a comfortable flat in one of the modern blocks on the central avenue. The day had begun early with a ring at the front door-bell and his wife had got up to answer it. Stavridis was Greek and it was only six o'clock. She had returned with a letter and Stavridis had read it. Chief Superintendent Bolton would be greatly obliged if Monsieur Stavridis could make it convenient to call on him at nine o'clock precisely.

Stavridis wrote an answer for the waiting Sikh constables. He would attend with great pleasure. Indeed he would, he privately thought. He could do rather more than guess at what Bolton would ask of him: he'd ask him to find Ernest, and that was quite in order provided the request were left simply at locating him. One wasn't chief spy for nothing. Besides, Ernest had caused trouble enough—first Madame, then a murder, finally a face-losing disturbance last night. It was better that Bolton should deal with him than that the formal request which was otherwise inevitable should be made to the shaikh to arrest him and hand him over, if indeed his men dared do it. In any case His Highness wouldn't fancy the request at all. Stavridis still held his original opinion that Ernest was His Highness's bed boy and it wasn't inconceivable that the shaikh would make difficulties. Even if he didn't he would certainly prevaricate and the pressure would fall on Stavridis. Who detested all forms of pressure unless he was applying them. Whereas if he went to Bolton he'd have something to *sell*. Not for money perhaps, but there were other things than money, and the presence in the shaikhdom of Major Mortimer of the Executive hadn't escaped Stavridis. He had a high opinion of the Executive and he hadn't always worked for Ali. Nor did he always mean to. This shaikhdom would disintegrate, sooner rather than later, and a friend at a court as powerful as the Executive would be an asset without price. Stavridis knew that if the chips went down Bolton and Mortimer could probably force him to do what at first they would simply ask for, but he had no intention of obliging them to force him. This wasn't that sort of game at all: on the contrary he had something to sell they wanted, and that was a situation which any Greek worth his salt could handle.

Stavridis dressed cheerfully and sent for his car, and he was drinking his coffee when the door-bell rang again. This time he went himself. It wasn't another letter but His Highness's personal servant. He had imperative instructions and he delivered them imperatively. Stavridis was to attend His Highness. At nine o'clock precisely.

He wasn't too worried. The change of time was an inconvenience, but there might even be an advantage in knowing something of Shaikh Ali's mind before he faced Bolton. He sent his dutiful obedience to the shaikh, then telephoned to Bolton; he said without evasion that he'd been summoned to his employer. If Chief Superintendent Bolton would excuse him till one hour later. . . . Yes, that was kind. Then at ten without fail. . . . His car had arrived and he drove to the palace. At most it was three hundred yards, but Stavridis wouldn't walk a foot when he'd a car on an expense account. With much less ceremony than was usual he was shown to the shaikh's study.

Stavridis saw at once that the shaikh's reluctant daemon had, for the moment, gripped him; he didn't invite the Greek to sit but began to talk crisply. Stavridis had a pendulous lower lip uncharacteristic of his race, and now it drooped in astonishment. When the shaikh had finished he said uncertainly: 'But Your Highness can't do this.'

'Why not?'

'You can't just *leave* us.'

'You mean leave *you*. But I assure you I can.'

Stavridis didn't answer. Come to that, he was thinking, he hadn't one. The shaikh possessed three million pounds, three million reasons to leave if he wished to. And on reflection it might be sensible. Stavridis would have bolted if he'd been in the shaikh's shoes—he would, that is, if he'd owned three million pounds. He temporized.

'And I'm to bring Ernest here to you?'

'That's what I told you.'

Stavridis thought it silly. The world was full of Ernest-men and some of them were prettier. He said with an undertone of genuine disapproval: 'It's a terrible risk to bring him here. After last night Bolton will have patrols out. He'll ring the city though he won't dare go hunting in it.'

'It's a risk *you're* going to run, my friend. Not me.'

'But why Ernest of all men?'

'Because I don't happen to drive a car. Because I'd trust him in mutual trouble.'

'I can drive,' the Greek said.

'I gave you a second reason for wanting Ernest.' The shaikh rose from his chair. He was wearing his robes again, aware of their authority. 'I can give you an hour exactly.' His hand fell on his dagger-hilt. 'After that. . . .'

'Your Highness, I'll do my best.'

'You'd be well advised to do so.'

Stavridis went back to his car and thought; he was on the horns squarely. Fail Bolton and Bolton could make his life intolerable: fail the shaikh and he might not have one. That hand on the dagger hadn't been meaningless. Stavridis had served Shaikh Ali well and in the process had made enemies. The shaikh, in addition, had other loyal servants. Bolton could annoy him but he was very unlikely to kill. Very well then, Shaikh Ali came first.

The decision had had an Attic simplicity but the next was more difficult. He'd been told to find Ernest and he'd been given an hour to do so. The hour didn't worry him, since if he could discover at all where Ernest was it would have to be quickly or never. It would be impossible for him to play hide-and-seek in the city, just as it was for Bolton and his alien Sikhs. But Stavridis knew that Ernest had been hiding in his mistress's house and he doubted if he'd gone back there. A woman's outer clothing had been found in the garden of the hotel and it was very long odds that Ernest had been using it. So it was also long odds that he'd spotted the beggar watching him—why otherwise disguise himself? So he'd hardly go back to a house he was known to be using.

Where else could he go to? Stavridis had just one line, and, he thought grimly, it had better be the right one. There'd been a near-riot in the square the night before and every indication that its beginnings at least had been organized. By Ernest, of course. And a man had been shot while trying to snatch a weapon from a policeman. Stavridis had had him checked at once—that he'd had work in the hotel and where he lived. But snatching a policeman's rifle wasn't local form at all; it was an action of courage and brave men weren't common. Which meant that Ernest could know this man, he'd conceivably even trust him. Which meant in turn that he'd know his house, he might even have gone to hole up there.

It was a guess but not a stupid one. Stavridis smiled

wanly—it had better be right or else. He gave his driver two addresses. At the first he picked up two men on his payroll, at the second he halted the car. It was the house of the Arab the Sikh had shot.

The car had been stopped as they swung from the central avenue and a havildar of police had checked the boot, then waved them on into the warren of the Arab town. Now they were deep in its fetid womb, halted before a crumbling tenement. Stavridis's two men went quietly in and he waited outside as quietly. His native bounce was returning, the sense that his gods were with him. If Ernest was there he'd have to come, for Stavridis had him dead stone cold. There was unlikely to be violence since nothing could be gained by it, and he had briefed his two men carefully both what to say and how to. . . . Ernest could come to Shaikh Ali's palace and there he could take such chance as offered. If he refused the result would be simple—simpler. No attempt would be made to force him, but Stavridis would drive straight to Bolton's office. With information, naturally, of where Ernest was now hiding.

When there wouldn't be a chance at all.

Stavridis waited confidently; he wasn't even relieved when Ernest appeared between his own two men. Ernest looked at Stavridis with an expression which told him nothing, then climbed into the car without a word. Without being told to he lay down on the floor. They covered him and ran for it. At the edge of the city a policeman half-challenged them, then his arm moved on and upwards into the stiffest of salutes. He was a Sikh and not intelligent, and Stavridis's car flew the shaikh's household flag.

Stavridis took his hat off, bowing back graciously. He'd watched the royal dukes of England on the cinema and telly.

They were brought before Shaikh Ali again and again he left them standing. There were armed men in a row behind him now. The shaikh said pleasantly: 'Good morning, Ernest.'

'Good morning, sir.' He had called the shaikh Highness exactly once and had promptly been told that sir would do.

'I've a job which I'd like you to do for me. You can drive me to the frontier.'

'I didn't know I was still your chauffeur, sir.'

'I don't remember dismissing you.'

Ernest said quietly: 'You sent me to England and in England——'

'In England you embroil yourself in some hare-brained scheme I've heard about. So they run you out and quite right too. Are you blaming me for that?'

'No. But when I get back here——'

'When you get back here I'd have saved myself trouble by having you killed at once.'

Ernest didn't answer and the shaikh turned away from him. He was a shrewd judge of character, Ernest's especially, for he had played much chess with him. Time to reflect was more likely to move him than a barrage of further argument. The shaikh waited patiently and Ernest thought. He'd never hated Shaikh Ali. He was an imperialist lackey, a ruthless exploiter of a people he cared nothing for, and as such he should be loathed and shunned. But Ernest had never done so. Ali wasn't a bad man at all, he'd been mostly considerate and often generous. Even packing a suspect chauffeur off to England had been a great deal less deadly than the solution most oil shaikhs would have reached for automatically. Of course this was very wrong thinking: what counted was the principle, never, but never, the man. And 'thinking' was too lenient—this was personal feeling, the crudest emotion. . . .

Heresy and fatal.

Yes, but if Ali once left the shaikhdom the possibilities would be unlimited. Better than killing Vincent Gale, better than some half-baked riot. The British would be forced to act, there'd be war or at least the threat of it, an international crisis. . . .

Anarchy—he'd been trained for it. His stern face broke suddenly into the smile of a fellow conspirator. 'I'll take you to the frontier, sir.'

'Good.' The shaikh snapped his fingers and two of his retainers detached themselves from the others; he said to Stavridis: 'You know too much and you know too soon. You'll have to be taken care of.'

Stavridis shivered. So his gods had deserted him, fickle as the race which had once fired their altars. It had been his amiable intention to drive straight from the palace to Geoffrey Bolton with the news that the shaikh was flitting, for with Ali gone there'd be only one master in the shaikhdom. Stavridis was courtier as well as spy, and masters were always people to propitiate. The king is dead, long live the king.

He shivered again as the shaikh watched him coolly; he'd gone paler than the Nordics he despised. Then he threw himself on his knees, arching his back, his hands before his face as though in prayer. It was a Levantine gesture and wholly horrible. He began to blubber noisily. 'Don't kill me, I've served you well. I . . . Don't kill me.'

'In the name of your God get up, Greek.' Ali sounded irritable but in fact he was not; he was utterly disgusted. This degrading abasement somehow involved him in the other's degradation; he said contemptuously: 'On your feet, man.'

'You're not going to kill me?'

'I'm not the killing kind, alas. Sometimes I wish I were.' The shaikh turned to the two retainers. 'Take this man away,' he said. 'Lock him up for an hour at least.' He looked back at Ernest. 'Well?'

'Have you packed, sir?'

'The minimum.'

'Then we're going alone?'

'We are.' The shaikh hid a smile in his handsome beard.

It had occurred to him that protocol demanded that he take at least a senior wife with him but he had put the thought behind him with some relief. They'd had it good while he'd been with them and he'd left them a little money. Besides, he wasn't rich; he had three million pounds and he could manage on that with care. But not with all those boring women.

Ernest said thoughtfully: 'Even without the Greek they'll hear we're leaving.'

'Yes, but not quite so soon.'

'You think they'll try and stop us, sir? They'll chase?'

'It's possible.' Shaikh Ali's smile was open now. 'That was one reason I asked you to come with me.'

'I see.' Ernest reflected, taking his time to do so; at last he said: 'But I'm sorry I'm quite unarmed, sir.'

Ali pointed at the bodyguard. 'Choose,' he said briefly.

Ernest did so professionally. He took an automatic rifle and three twenties of ammunition.

Geoffrey Bolton put back the telephone grimly. Mortimer had been listening on the extension. Bolton looked at his watch. 'They've twenty-five minutes start,' he said.

'But a pretty old car.'

'Should we take Gale? He's our boss in a sense.'

'He'll be down at the airport and almost off. We'll have him stopped if there's still time to do it, but we can't afford to wait for him.' Bolton scribbled a note. 'Let's go, then.'

'Right.'

They ran to the car outside.

Chapter Eleven

Vincent Gale was sitting in the aircraft waiting for take-off and the reaction which he'd been fearing had engulfed him. He should, he supposed, have been feeling furious: Madame had treated him abominably, throwing him out like some impertinent inferior. Resentment, even anger were the appropriate emotions. Instead he felt miserable, regretting that he'd lost her; he'd been successful as a Minister but he'd failed wretchedly as a man. And his ill-temper wasn't mitigated by the aircraft's delay. Another airline would have explained things, at least have given an estimate of how long there was still to wait, but he'd been left twenty minutes in a temperature round the hundred, and beyond the original grudging announcement that there was an unavoidable delay nobody had deigned to speak again. It was all very English and Gale was sweating.

He had noticed the jeep but had paid it small attention. It seemed to be going extremely fast, and so it damned well should, he thought. This would be the mail perhaps, more likely the pilot's laundry. He'd forgotten and sent back for it, he'd kept them all waiting. . . . Gale watched the jeep irritably. It was cutting across the runways, ploughing through sand between them, pitching unsteadily. Through the dust which encompassed it Gale could make out two Sikhs, one driving, one waving at the pilot with an urgency Gale could feel. The jeep drove under the starboard wing braking hard by the fuselage. The gangway was half a mile away, left behind when they'd taxi-ed out, but the jeep had a folding ladder. A ruffled steward opened the door, the ladder came up at him, and well before he had made it fast a Sikh had climbed aboard. He looked around, locating Gale; he saluted and gave him a paper.

It was Bolton's scribble, six lines at most, but it shook Gale instantly from the lethargy of depression. He ran to the aircraft's door, sliding down the ladder as carelessly as a boy. The black dog had left him, he felt confident, almost gay. They might stop the shaikh or again they might not. On the whole Gale thought not. In either case there'd be work to do, proper work and he meant to do it. He said to the driver: 'To the Princess Nahid's. Never mind the precautions. Go.'

'But sahib, your luggage——'

'Go.'

Half an hour later the great door was opening. Gale fretted while the procession formed though he didn't try to jump it. But he walked into Madame at what was almost a trot. She rose to him in astonishment and also, he saw, in the same black rage. Vincent Gale ignored it, asking with an authority which he knew was the last mood expected: 'Have they told you the news?'

'If you mean about my brother—yes.' She was struggling for self-control again. 'So you fixed him,' she said savagely, 'you've driven him out. And now you've come back to gloat at me.'

'You're not usually unintelligent. Why should I want to gloat?' He'd decided to shock her and saw that he had. But she was still fighting back.

'You're that sort of man.'

'I am when I want to be. I am when I've something to

gloat over. But just at the moment I'm in the same boat as you are.'

She considered it reluctantly. 'Are you telling me you'd no part in this?'

'Of course I am.'

'Then why are you here?'

'I thought you might welcome an ally.'

She was silent while he watched her rage dissolve in an evident doubt; at length she said: 'But you were talking about the Cabinet, not being able to stay here and——'

'I was. There's something called collective responsibility, though it's taken a knock or two recently.' He laughed at her astonishment. 'I think I could stay a day or two without straining the constitution. Now that I've a motive to.'

'But what?'

'Ali's bolting, of course. Apart from that, try looking in the looking glass.'

She took another long silence and at its end said reasonably: 'But it was Ernest was the the trouble-maker and with Ernest gone with Ali. . . .'

'With Ernest gone there may still be trouble. Not the same sort of trouble but maybe worse. I think——'

In the courtyard there was a sudden commotion.

There was no made road to the frontier post since for fifty weeks of the fifty-two none was necessary, and the cost of an all-weather highway for the remaining two would have been a sum which Shaikh Ali would certainly have considered wasted on anything as public as a road. Instead there were tracks, several running parallel, following the line of old-fashioned wooden telegraph poles. They were dusty and rutted, death to the springing of the stoutest car, but except in the fortnight of a doubtful and reluctant rain were passable. The twenty miles they traversed were hell on earth—flat, waterless and abandoned. The heat snatched your breath away.

They had taken the convertible and Ernest was driving carefully. He knew that pursuit was possible, for they had left with luggage and Bolton would have informers, but the car wasn't new and a broken spring would surrender the advantage which he also knew he took with him. It was an advantage of time, though he didn't know how much of it, but more important it was one of initiative too. He had an automatic rifle and it was likely that any pursuers would have pistols at least. But he could shoot freely and they could not —not at a target which included the shaikh. Ernest had made his decision: if anyone came after them he'd stick tight with the car and Ali. He could fire at his discretion but they'd think twice before returning it.

He drove on steadily, watching the mileage on the trip of the speedometer. Eighteen, nineteen, a mile to go. . . .

It was Shaikh Ali who saw it first, the pillar of dust which was the inescapable companion of any vehicle in the desert. He said conversationally: 'There's something behind us, by the dust going fast.'

Ernest looked in the driving mirror. The dust was two miles behind and it was one to the frontier.

. . . Run for it or stand and shoot?

The shaikh read his thoughts. 'If we knew we could drive straight through——' he said.

'You think we could?'

'I'm afraid we can't. There'll be formalities and a lot of words.'

Ernest didn't answer him. He stopped the car, still facing forward, taking the rifle, climbing across the driver's seat and into the rear compartment. He knelt on the cushion, steadying the automatic on the folded hood. Shaikh Ali he kept behind him.

Ali said pleasantly: 'Forgive me the repetition but I'm not the killing kind.'

'I don't think I'll have to kill them, sir.'

Ernest was watching the cloud of dust as the other car

came closer. Their own dust was settling and in any other circumstances that would have left them naked. Now, he thought briefly, it hardly mattered. He put the rifle to single shot, the sights to a hundred and fifty. He waited impassively.

At three hundred yards he could make out two men and at a hundred and fifty he fired a shot. He'd been shooting for the windscreen and he'd got it. He'd been aiming for the centre but one man had slumped. Then he came back in sight again. The car came on.

. . . By God, they're not cowards.

Ernest switched to automatic fire, lowering the muzzle, firing a long burst at the offside tyre. He saw at once that he hadn't missed. The car swung to the right, the driver wrestling with the kicking wheel. Ernest saw it was Geoffrey Bolton. He was out of control. . . . No. . . . Yes. . . .

The car hit a rut in another track, rearing alarmingly, spinning on its axis through a hundred and eighty degrees. With an air almost of reluctance it slowly keeled over.

Both men had jumped clear of it, running towards Ernest. They were shouting something he couldn't hear but they weren't waving firearms. He reloaded expertly and fired two more bursts, one well to the right, the other left. The two men dropped but they didn't fire.

Ernest climbed back into the driver's seat, watching the prone men across his shoulder. They hadn't moved. Ali said formally: 'I thank you Ernest.'

'It seems I'm still your chauffeur, sir.'

They drove on towards the frontier.

The shaikh's intention had been straightforward. There was a little town beyond the frontier and the end of a metregauge railway. Ali had steadfastly refused its extension across his own territory since his relations with his vastly more powerful neighbour were something short of cordial. But they weren't so bad that he could conceivably be held as hostage: on the contrary his neighbour would co-operate in a flight which would certainly suit his book. His neighbour would lick his bearded chops, then await his own advantage from the collapse of the shaikhdom. So Shaikh Ali would take train to the capital and there he'd hire an aircraft. He'd known for years where he wanted to go and decidedly not to Switzerland.

Ali had left orders that the frontier post be telephoned half an hour after Ernest and he had slipped unostentatiously from a back entrance to the palace, and on arrival the commander received him formally. He himself had had time to telephone to his capital—Ali had intended it—and his instructions had been clear. He was to admit the shaikh and to put himself at his disposal.

He was doing so now in a good deal of flowery Arabic. If he'd heard firing he didn't mention it. On a frontier one didn't. Ali listened politely while the luggage was taken over. There was a train in an hour and His Highness could be accommodated. Not properly, the notice had been too short, but if speed was more important than the comfort to which His Highness was entitled. . . .

Shaikh Ali said emphatically it was and the commander fussed away. Ernest was standing quietly, a little apart, and the shaikh walked towards him. He hadn't spoken since the shooting and Ali had respected his silence. Ernest was pale —strained, Ali thought, to breaking. He said to him now: 'You can take the car back. That is, if you want to.'

'Very good, sir.'

'But if you'd care to come over I'll see you're not left penniless.'

'No thank you, sir.'

The shaikh said deliberately: 'They'll get you, you know.'

'I'm not optimistic either.' Ernest smiled on the words but faintly.

'I beg you to be sensible. I know what you are and so will the British. The British aren't fools and this is oil.'

'It's also opportunity.'

'My—my abdication, you mean?' The shaikh answered his own question. 'But I didn't believe you'd driven me here for love.' Shaikh Ali shrugged. 'Well, there's one thing I can do for you—no, not money, you've made that clear. You wouldn't take a gift from me and that I can understand. I wouldn't take money either if our positions were reversed. However. . . .'

The shaikh pulled out a notebook and started to write in it. He wrote at first from right to left, in Arabic, then shook his head. 'A beautiful language, the language to talk to God in, but alas, imprecise.' He wrote again in English, tearing the page out and handing it to Ernest. It wasn't an English he often wrote, but it had the resonance and something of the authority of the original draft in Arabic.

To whomsoever it may concern
I, Ali bin Hasan bin Ibrahim, commend to your duty the bearer of this certificate, Ernest or Ernst, my servant. He who may oblige him obliges also myself and may address himself accordingly for the discharge of the obligation.

Shaikh Ali had signed in Arabic. Ernest read it impassively and put it in his wallet.

The shaikh said with a sudden emphasis: 'It isn't quite useless if that's what you're thinking. I'm leaving so I'm no longer shaikh, but I'm still head of the family and that I'll take with me. I'll be leaving behind relations and friends. Relations especially.'

'I wasn't thinking that, sir.'

'Then?'

'I was wondering why you bother.'

'You were quite a good chess player.' Shaikh Ali's voice went down a tone. 'And you're also a very brave man.' The shaikh turned on his heel. 'Farewell,' he said.

He didn't look back—he was weeping unashamedly. He walked towards the barrier in the long wire fence.

As the shaikh walked away from him Ernest raised the rifle. He'd put it at single shot again for a single shot would do it. In the back, left side. The heart.

. . . Anarchy—he'd been trained for it. If the shaikh left the shaikhdom the possibilities would be unlimited. But he could always come back or the British might bring him. Whereas a pressure on the trigger. . . .

Ernest, very slowly, let the rifle slide downwards. He walked to the car and drove furiously away in it.

He'd failed again—he knew it. And this was worse than mere failure, it was betrayal of what he stood for.

It was sin.

He drove crazily to escape from it.

Outside Madame's door there was a sudden commotion. The princess went to it, returning with a paper. It was another half sheet and Gale read it quickly. Bolton and Mortimer had been pinned by fire from an automatic weapon a bare mile from the frontier. They'd been armed but quite impotent—they hadn't dared shoot at a car with the shaikh in it. Twenty minutes later the shaikh's car had returned past the wreck of their own, but keeping its distance; there'd been only one man in it and he'd been driving like a maniac. Bolton and Mortimer had walked to the frontier and had telephoned from there. Ali had crossed so the man in the car had been Ernest. By now he'd have dumped it, probably in the harbour, and have lost himself in the bazaar again. And now he had a rifle. Bolton had hired another car and both men were coming back in it.

Gale said collectedly: 'We were talking about your brother and we'd got as far as Ernest. I was wrong about Ernest.'

'How?'

'Ernest came back again. You must excuse me now but I'll ring you this evening.'

'But——'

'I can see you don't quite trust me.' He smiled unexpectedly. 'I told you what to do,' he said. 'Look in a looking glass.' He took her hand and kissed it; he was gone.

For perhaps a minute Madame stood motionless, then she walked to a mirror obediently. It answered her as a woman would and the answer was reassuring. She began to laugh softly. She'd been offered an alliance—hell. Alliance was a bigwig's word, a word for a Foreign Secretary. She wasn't interested in Ministers but Vincent Gale had impressed her. She'd kicked him out like a dog and he'd come back at her like, like . . .

Like, she decided, a man she'd underestimated. She felt no regret, no necessity to excuse herself: what she felt was pure pleasure. They'd be meeting again and that was good.

. . . Alliance indeed! Pronounce it a little differently and it meant something entirely different.

Chapter Twelve

Twenty-four hours later an alliance of quite a different kind was being courteously mooted in the Security Executive in London. Colonel Charles Russell was accustomed to unusual visitors who, in his experience, had ranged from eminent persons whose hobbies had brought them into conflict with the more archaic survivals on the statute book and would be grateful—pathetically grateful—if Russell would use his influence with the police, to ladies who had been treated despitefully by the foreign diplomatists whom he had suggested they should cultivate to their mutual advantage and profit. He had formulae for both of these, polite regret for the first class, handsome and uncovenanted payments to the second, but he hadn't a formula for a visit by the head of the security services of a formally unfriendly state.

Russell had had some difficulty in securing the lean General's entry into England at all. The Foreign Office had been offended that the object of the visit had been openly stated as a talk with Colonel Russell: a visitor of General rank should be presented by his ambassador and to a junior Minister at least. There was more than a hint of unseemly hurry and the Foreign Office detested hurries. Charles Russell had dealt with that by the expedient of ignoring it; he knew where the real decision lay whether the lean man should or should not visit him, and that wasn't in the Foreign Office, far less with the Home Secretary, whom the proposal had stricken with a predictable alarm. Russell had access and Russell had used it. He would not, he had explained, talk politics; he would not wish to even if the lean man did, and Russell was sure he didn't. But in the secret war between two systems of intelligence there was bound to be neutral ground, and where there was neutrality there could also be advantage. Russell had been listened to and asked a single question. He had answered it simply and the Prime Minister had nodded. . . . The General would be admitted as a perfectly private person. So keep me in touch. Good luck.

Now the lean man was sitting in the Security Executive, talking in fluent and slightly old-fashioned English. And, Russell thought, not the less clear for that. The General was saying politely: 'It's kind of you to receive me and I hope I haven't surprised you. But in a world where the two most powerful men alive can talk to each other by teletype perhaps it isn't quite extraordinary that simple officials like you and me should wish to get together.'

'You're very welcome indeed, sir.'

'I hope you'll think so when I've finished. If this were an ordinary Department I'd have sent you a paper first. A committee would have considered it and you and I got nowhere. But since I haven't done that I'll have to define my terms of reference. That means in plain English that I'll tell you what game we propose to play. My limits, in fact . . . I hope I'm not boring you?'

'No.' Russell spoke without irony. He had more than one matter to fear of the lean man but boredom wasn't one of them.

'I'm very much obliged. Then I ought to say at once that we haven't gone soft. One of my superiors made a crack about burying you——'

'We've heard various glosses of that.'

'My advice is to ignore them. It's still an article of faith with us that one day our system will smother yours. We accept the cold war and we're certain to win it. But you're too intelligent to suppose that anarchy is invariably a pleasing spectacle to a communist but European Power. In a nuclear and increasingly Balkanized world we've sometimes an interest in avoiding the Sarajevos, or at least in containing their repercussions.'

'Which I take as a friendly warning that though you'll destroy us you'll pick your time. And place.'

The General said warmly: 'You're a very real pleasure to talk to. May I take you up on "place"?'

'Of course.'

'Then this shaikhdom is an example. It might suit us to see you lose the oil—you see I'm returning your candour—but we've never believed that you'd lose it entirely feebly. Moreover it isn't all yours by any means and you've a powerful and dangerous ally. We simply can't afford that this tuppenny-ha'penny shaikhdom should escalate into another major confrontation. There's a possible advantage in denying you oil but we gamble by the book. The odds simply aren't good enough.'

'But some friends of yours think differently.'

'Of course they do—their interests are wholly different. Another Albania in the shaikhdom would be a triumph ideologically, the shaikhdom itself is a great deal more important to the West than Albania, and finally it would be a slap in the face to ourselves. But we're not interested in oil-shaikhs, or not, I should say, for the moment. You follow me?'

'Perfectly. Islands seem to be your current speciality. One gone, one cooking, and then, I'd say, Cyprus. Perhaps Ceylon next.'

'That's a little beyond my present visit.' There was the faintest emphasis on 'present'. The lean man accepted a cigarette. 'May I ask you a question?'

'About the shaikhdom? Certainly.'

'The instrument of what you called some friends of ours is a revolutionary called Ernst.' The General smiled. 'I believe you have knowledge of Ernst.'

'I've been meaning to thank you for that.'

It was waved aside. 'I've been thinking for a long time that I'd do well to come and talk to you. What was decisive was the news they woke me with late last night that the shaikh had made a bolt for it. Even more alarming that your Foreign Secretary had cancelled his passage back to London and apparently meant to stay on indefinitely. I thought that was serious, time that we met. So we radioed our embassy here in terms you'll surely know about and I got straight on an aircraft to talk about Ernst. Four hours in the air but your clocks save me three of them.'

'You haven't lost time,' Charles Russell said.

'I don't when it seems important. And returning to Ernst I've an obvious question first. He's managed to fix a near-riot and he's murdered a junior Minister. Why don't you simply erase him?'

'I would if I could.'

'Could . . . ? But he's a single man against the Security Executive.' The lean man sounded incredulous.

'But a man with an advantage. He's hiding in the native town, slipping from one hide-out to another, and any attempt to comb the bazaar runs a real risk of starting exactly the sort of trouble he'd give his eyes to achieve himself. I don't say we couldn't do it, indeed we may well be forced to, but we take the risk seriously.'

The lean General reflected. 'I didn't know that. I see. But with the Foreign Secretary staying on in the shaikhdom——'

'If you'd care to say I'm a worried man I wouldn't contradict you. It's really extremely irregular.'

Irregular, Charles Russell thought, but interesting too. The orthodox action would be for the Foreign Secretary to return at once, consult with his colleagues, then issue orders through the machinery of Whitehall. Vincent Gale was hardly a champion of the orthodox for its own sake but he'd be certain to take the simple course unless he had reason not to. *Ergo* a reason existed and politically it was less than obvious. But politics apart, personal motive, the human 'x', was the jam on the bread and butter of the Executive's daily routine. There was Madame no doubt, but Madame's private interests could be protected from London just as easily as from the shaikhdom and her personal safety if there was trouble there was hardly a charge on a middle-aged Foreign Secretary.

No, but it might be on Vincent Gale. Russell remembered that though he respected the Foreign Secretary he wouldn't have sworn he liked him. There was something about him, a certain detachment, on the surface a certain lack.

Russell stirred in his chair. Mr. Vincent Gale. . . . He'd meet obligations but emotions he wouldn't spend. More precisely he hadn't so far. This was interesting indeed and Russell would sleep on it happily. Just for the moment the lean man was talking again, recapitulating quickly.

'So if I've understood rightly you're caught between two fires. You can't arrest Ernst without risking the sort of trouble which would force you into action highly damaging to you internationally—calling troops in, I imagine, and looking like the colonialists we should certainly say you were. And very loudly indeed—that's part of the general game, you know, though not the one we're playing here. Alternatively so long as your Minister stays in the shaikhdom there's an evident risk from an Ernst at large. I can't assess it, that's your business not mine, but it's clear that if he murdered him you couldn't simply ignore it. So troops again, take the wretched place over, but howls from the League, the face of great Powers, threats, *escalation*. . . .' The General frowned. 'Not there,' he said, 'not for some shaikh when we've a surplus of oil ourselves. *Not now*. That's why I'm here.' He was suddenly emphatic. 'But so long as Gale stays there we're both at risk equally.'

'I can't recall Mr. Vincent Gale. The Cabinet could if he stayed too long but he's a very powerful Minister. If he chooses to stay there a week, let's say, I think he might get away with it.'

'As one professional to another . . . ?'

'This morning's aircraft to the shaikhdom was full of first-class men of mine.'

'Of course. Forgive me the question.' There was a minute of reflection through most of a second cigarette. 'Then perhaps we could help.'

'If it comes to erasement we can wash our own linen.'

'As, if I may say so, I've observed. No, I was thinking of something less violent.' The lean man was silent again, stubbing the cigarette; at last he said: 'Suppose *Ernst* were recalled. Suppose his masters withdrew him.'

It was Russell's turn to sound faintly incredulous. 'You think you could contrive it?'

'I think it's worth a try. Our relations with what you call our friends are notably short of friendly, but I wasn't considering asking a favour. We haven't been sending them arms for years but there's something we still supply them with which they couldn't face losing.' The General shrugged. 'I can't decide myself, of course—I'll have to talk to my superiors—but if I persuade them that Ernst is big enough, a big enough threat to what they see as our present interests. . . .'

'The squeeze would go on?'

'It would indeed.'

'And what,' Russell asked, 'do I pay for this?'

'Nothing, *cher collègue*—nothing for the moment.' There was a sardonic chuckle, entirely Slav. 'Let's say that I'm opening an account with the Security Executive and that for the moment I'm content with the credit entry. And now if you'll excuse me I'll go back to our embassy and signal.' The General stood up. 'Tell me,' he said, 'as one official to another. Do you ever have hunches?'

'I often have wrong ones.'

'Alas, so do I. But just at this moment I've a pricking of my thumbs. That shaikhdom is really extremely hot. . . . I was going to fly back tomorrow, now I'll signal at once instead. Immediate.' The General held his hand out, smiling. 'I'm in credit—you'll remember?'

'To our next fruitful meeting, sir.'

It had been nearly midnight before Gale had telephoned to Madame. She had been first in his thoughts, but the essential keys to action lay with Bolton and Robert Mortimer. Mortimer had his arm in a sling from a flesh wound which he insisted hadn't damaged him; he had had, he explained, all the luck of the Executive. Gale had told him that he meant to stay—the shaikh's disappearance left the shaikhdom wide open and until proper arrangements could be made with London the Foreign Secretary must accept the responsibility which unexpectedly had been dropped on him. Mortimer had taken it without commenting directly but he'd insisted again that it wasn't only a question of the shaikh having run for it: Ernest had also returned with arms, and Ernest's intention had been to murder Vincent Gale. The Executive was responsible for his safety and Mortimer must contact Russell immediately. One man had been enough before but now it clearly wasn't.

Robert Mortimer hadn't been happy, but Gale had realized that along with his apprehension went a certain relief to balance it. And Bolton shared it equally. Both men were competent but neither a politician, and the situation now developing was inexorably political. The shaikh had flitted and Ernest was back; the Resident had sailed away; the Agent in trouble would be out of his league; and on the rising graph of violence the next outbreak might be irreparable. Bolton had suggested, politely but firmly, that Gale move to his house at once since his personal protection there would be easier than at the hotel. Mortimer had backed him, and it was from Bolton's pleasant old bungalow that Gale had telephoned to Madame. Now he was saying with a briskness he didn't feel: 'The plane I was on has gone of course, but there's another tomorrow and I've booked you a seat on it. At nine o'clock. Does that give you time to pack?'

'Pack what?'

'What you'll want for the journey.'

'What journey?'

'A trip to London. Or to Nice if you prefer it.'

'And why should I go to London?'

'Hell. . . .' It was the question he'd been expecting and he hadn't a proper answer—not to the Princess Nahid. Who should have been her father's son. He'd been bluffing and she'd called it but he ought to try again. It was certain to sound feeble but——

'It may get pretty rough down here.'

'Is that a promise? Mostly it's simply boring.'

He said patiently but not hopefully: 'But just suppose there *were* trouble—what could you do?'

'I could watch the Foreign Secretary in action.'

'You've used that crack before.'

'Listen,' she said, 'I'm Ali's sister. I'm also not the running kind. What exactly do you anticipate?'

'I wish I knew.'

'Some action against myself?'

'It's clearly possible. You're Ali's sister, rather a forceful woman and——'

'Then why not send some police up here? I wouldn't object to a bodyguard.'

'If you care to look out you'll see them.'

'So?' Madame sounded interested. 'Then you've been talking to Geoffrey Bolton. That man attracts me.'

'But seriously——'

'Vincent,' she said, 'it's time you grew up.' The words were reproving, the voice warm as milk—tolerant, he decided, as domestic as knitting. They might have been married for twenty years. She went on smoothly. 'Where are you now?'

'At Bolton's with Major Mortimer.'

'I've heard good of Major Mortimer. Bring him to see me and don't forget the policeman.' She was mocking him again. 'And come to lunch tomorrow, quite alone. Can you eat omelettes?'

'I can eat a good omelette.'

'I do them beautifully.'

Chapter Thirteen

Charles Russell escorted the lean General to the car which his embassy had provided for him, then returned to his desk to draft a cable. He would send it Most Immediate, though it was a classification which he used sparingly, resenting its depreciation at the hands of incontinent colleagues. But this was genuinely urgent. He had told the General that the morning plane for the shaikhdom had been full of first-class men of his, and though this had been a colloquialism it was a fact that five experienced men had been collected, briefed and then dispatched in the interval between the arrival of Mortimer's signal the night before and the departure of the morning flight. It had been a considerable feat of organization, comparable, Russell thought smiling, to the decision and speed of the General's own dash to London. But at the moment he wasn't congratulating himself, since the five men had carried a letter to Mortimer which must now be modified. Before the General's call on him Russell had been concerned for the safety of Vincent Gale against an Ernest returned and armed. That danger would remain so long as both Gale and Ernest stayed together in the shaikhdom, but if the General's plan was successful Ernest would soon be leaving it. It was therefore essential to give the General time to make his own arrangements.

Russell drafted carefully, conscious that he was in no position to give formal orders. To Mortimer, yes—his previous instructions had been that if Bolton so wished it Russell's reinforcements might be used not only to guard Gale personally but also (of course discreetly) in the arrest of Ernest. But it would be Bolton's decision still and he must make it on all the facts; he must be told at once that there was now the possibility that Ernest would be withdrawn from the shaikhdom without the necessity of arresting him and therefore without risking the disturbance in the native town which was always entailed in doing so. Charles Russell smiled again. That possibility lay in the hands of a foreign General, one who had called him, but quite without irony, *cher collègue*.

Russell wrote smoothly but without the firm imperatives which he would have used if he had been able to. He was not. He could advise Geoffrey Bolton and obliquely he was doing so, but he could not give him orders. . . . It was Colonel Russell's opinion that there was at least a case for waiting a week before chancing the dangers which even a limited sally into the bazaar would make inevitable, and with five trained men to call on Gale's personal safety couldn't be in question while they waited. Nevertheless the decision must be Bolton's.

This, Russell knew, was only formally true, correct as between one official and another. The real decision would be the Foreign Secretary's, but Vincent Gale was a Queen's Counsel, Ernest a murderer, and the proposition at bottom was that a murderer should be allowed to go lest his arrest involve a riot or worse. Politically it was a valid deal but there was also a lawyer's conscience. But Russell wouldn't have laid much money on the Foreign Secretary's decision. Vincent Gale, and increasingly, would be a dangerous man to bet on. The fact that he'd stayed in the shaikhdom at all. . . .

Charles Russell shrugged; he signed his telegram and sent it. He had added that the Prime Minister had been informed.

It arrived late that evening and Mortimer brought it to

Vincent Gale at once. Gale saw that it changed everything and he began, a little wearily, to draft another signal of his own. He seemed to have been sending them with unaccustomed frequency, for he had little patience with the Foreign Office habit of sending a telegram upon any excuse or none at all. . . . You don't know what to do, my dear—it's really a trifle sticky? Then send a telegram to the post of course. We can quietly ignore the answer but it'll always look well on the file. At least we've consulted the man on the spot. . . . What was that? But my dear, we're not the Treasury.

Gale's previous signals had been the reverse of these extravagances—lucid, a simple reporting of events as they had happened, with one immediate recommendation. There'd been a first the previous afternoon, the bare news from the airport that Ali had bolted, then, the same evening, when Bolton and Mortimer had returned from the frontier, a formal confirmation that he'd crossed it. The recommendation had been that the Resident and the Agent must be replaced immediately. Gale himself would remain and report next day in detail.

He had done so at tea-time after luncheon with Madame, though the fact that he'd consulted her wouldn't interest the Prime Minister and Gale therefore hadn't mentioned it, confining himself to the situation as it stood. Bolton and Mortimer had spent the morning with Stavridis, and Stavridis had been indecently, even obscenely, anxious to oblige them. So they knew Ernest's hide-out but not if he were there again. (Had Stavridis had any clue to that? No, no, he hadn't —really. He'd been shaking like a jelly and they'd believed him.)

So it wasn't quite certain where Ernest was but there was no other choice but to go for where he had been. Gale had authorized preparations, then eaten an omelette with the Princess Nahid. Who'd seemed surprisingly hesitant. . . . There were six of Charles Russell's men here now, and surely that was adequate to guard even a Foreign Secretary?

Gale had agreed that it was ample. Then weren't the risks of arresting Ernest still as great as ever? The Princess had stressed them—she knew them, none better. Some loutish Sikh had only to pull a curtain down, he might even do it by accident, and if there happened to be a woman behind there'd be knives out in no time. The whole town was tinder, and that sort of fire once started would need more than Bolton's Sikhs to put it out. Wasn't Gale, above all things, determined he wouldn't call troops in?

He had agreed again, but puzzled, explaining that there was now no question of an organized search. This would be a raid on a known address, Bolton and Mortimer were sensible steady men, and Bolton in particular had the experience to minimize any chance of affront. Besides, with five trained and, one hoped, traditionally phlegmatic Englishmen to replace those hated Sikhs the chances of an incident would be significantly reduced. Finally one couldn't leave a murderer un-arrested for ever. Gale thought without astonishment that once he would have put that first.

She had agreed at last though with a reluctance which had surprised him, and he had sent a third signal accordingly.

And now he had to cancel it, for he wholly agreed with Russell. Gale wrote his fourth message carefully; he was sending in the Agent's code but it wasn't a very high one.

PERSONAL TO PRIME MINISTER
from
GALE
IMMEDIATE
Have been informed by Security Executive of proposal made by senior foreign official Stop Understand you have been informed similarly Stop Suggest course outlined in my immediately preceding telegam be suspended for one week.

The reply came next morning and Gale read it appreciatively. The Prime Minister had the talent, rare in Whitehall, of writing its language but of using it with an accent as unmistakable as his speech. The words were formal and even stale but the Prime Minister came through strongly. He agreed that it would be sensible to allow a week before taking any irreversible action against Ernest. He'd even be willing to agree to rather longer, for it was his impression that since the flight of the shaikh Ernest was no longer the principal danger. That was the risk of invasion by a neighbour: even serious signs of it would make the dispatch of troops inevitable, and the Foreign Secretary would realize perfectly the repercussions which could follow. However, certain pressures had been put on Ali's neighbour and an essential ally had backed them strongly. The news was therefore reassuring. The shaikh himself was in Spain, in Cordoba it seemed, apparently buying a house there. The Prime Minister approved of that. A charming town and enchanting people. And the Military Attaché across the frontier had reported no troops moving. Repeat, the Military Attaché.

Vincent Gale had laughed aloud for the repetition hadn't been lost on him. The Military Attaché wasn't a diplomat *de carrière* and the Prime Minister was therefore trusting him to observe reliably anything as obvious as soldiers marching on a frontier.

Gale returned to the telegram. It was moving now into the rhetoric, but gentle and inoffensive, which was the trademark of the Prime Minister's private style. He'd written this one himself. . . . Did not Gale agree that since his failure to raise a serious riot this Ernest had shot his bolt? Was there not a possibility of seeing the situation a little too locally? (*Num*, was that, or *nonne*?) The replacement of the Resident and the immediate transfer of the Agent had already been recommended and accepted. That matter was well in hand. Then was this Ernest a threat so serious as to justify immobilizing the Foreign Secretary in the shaikhdom? The Prime Minister for one would welcome his counsel in London.

Vincent Gale had laughed again; he could recognize the

portents. This was a warning shot, polite, even stylized. The suggestion would come next, then maybe a stronger one. Finally the order, courteous but inescapable.

He gave himself three days before the crunch.

He wrote a noncommittal answer and was driven to Madame's house again.

The princess received him with the relaxed familiarity which he half enjoyed and half resented. Since their quarrel she'd been as good as gold—too good. He might have been her husband, admired perhaps and even loved, but treated with the unconscious tolerance of a woman whose marriage had been successful. She asked him now: 'Are you staying to lunch?'

'If it's omelettes again of course I am.'

They sat down to good coffee and cigarettes, and to the comfortable silence of an increasing ease. Gale said at length: 'I've been sending a lot of telegrams and this morning the boss replied to one.'

'The Prime Minister?'

He nodded. 'He wants me to go back again; he thinks I'm over-estimating Ernest's importance.'

'And I dare say he's right.' He looked at her, surprised, but she went on calmly: 'From his own point of view— from how it must look in London. Ernest's a revolutionary but it looks as though he's finished. It could have been serious that night you opened the Council, but that was the best chance he's had. How can he work another? You know how important prestige is here—success breeds success and vice versa. Much more so vice versa.'

'That's almost what the Prime Minister said.'

'Then clearly he isn't stupid. And as for your own safety you're arresting Ernest now. We agreed on that yesterday.'

'No, we're not arresting him. Not yet.'

'Why not?'

He told her and she whistled. 'You Europeans! You can

certainly close the ranks when it's anything that matters. Oil, for example. We don't stand a chance, we Arabs.' It was a statement of fact but Gale hid a smile. He glanced round the room. There were *marqueterie* furniture and an early Braque he coveted indecently. Her French was a Frenchwoman's and her English perfect. Arabs, indeed! He'd forgotten she was half one.

But she was speaking again. 'Then you mean to wait a week? And how will you use it?'

'In doing the obvious chores. I won't feel quite happy till there's a new Resident in headquarters and above all things a new Agent here. And we'll have to find Ali's heir.'

'I wish you good luck of him.'

It was a warning and he realized it, for the matter of the succession was an awkward one. Ali hadn't abdicated formally, and it wasn't inconceivable that he'd make difficulties about doing so. There were certainly lawyers who, suitably instructed, could make interminable trouble, and even if Ali's intention had been to quit cleanly, even if he confirmed it, there was still the embarrassment of a so far untraced successor. Gale asked her quietly: 'Have you ever met him?'

'No. I told you the position once—our blood's getting pretty thin. Ali was childless, and though he had a brother he died without sons too. That takes you back to my father's kin, and he wasn't one for having them hanging about. I had an uncle Saleh but he's almost certainly dead, and his son was called Sayyid. I've never even met him. Father had his defects, but having his relations sponging about his palace wasn't one of them. He was wise about that—just look across the frontier if you doubt it. Sayyid may be within the shaikhdom still but it's as likely he isn't. He may be a herdsman, he may be a clerk. He may be the subject of another and awkward state. He may be dead.'

'You think he'd come back to make his claim?'

'Good God yes, he's an Arab. But he may not hear for days or weeks. If he's in any sort of town he'll hear at once, but if he's gone back to desert life. . . .' She shrugged indifferently. There was nothing to be done but wait.

'And meanwhile?' Gale asked.

'You're lucky to have this Council-thing.'

'Yes-es.' He was hesitant and sounded it. 'It's not precisely experienced.'

'I know it's not. We quarrelled about it once and cleared the air. It's the shameless sham it always was—no, I'm not picking another fight. It's a silly façade but now it could be a useful one. You might even consider calling it a Council of Regency.'

'Three obsequious stooges plus four others to come? You don't seriously think the four to be elected will be different.'

'They could be if the right men stood.'

'Have we got them?' he asked.

The princess passed the plural without comment. 'I know one,' she said. 'Ernest.'

He didn't laugh or even wish to; instead he slid a glance at her through the smoke of her cigarette. She smoked without fuss, disdaining a holder or even tips, the cigarette drooping casually from the corner of her mouth. It was a *gamine* gesture, the reverse of a princess's, but the suggestion had had a regal steel. If she thought as once she'd said she did then Ernest would be a proper choice for Councillor. He'd destroy her inevitably but she might not care, and Gale could believe she didn't. She'd complained of British indifference with a passion wholly credible; she took two per cent of her brother's loot and she gave away half of it. The rest ran through a handful of bank accounts, out into the insatiable sands of a dozen rich men's cupidity. The British, it seemed, would stand for that: it was certain that Ernest wouldn't. Almost without weighing it he said: 'It's a pity he's a murderer.'

'Would that stop him doing what you don't care to?'

'Last time you said "don't dare to".'

'I don't want to quarrel again. One did us good but two's too many.'

138

'He's also a communist agent.'

'The agent scares both of us—I'm not quite a fool. The communist scares you, not me.'

There was a long silence of established intimacy. Gale was conscious of a commitment which surprised him. It wasn't a word he normally allowed. Novelists were committed when they couldn't sell their novels, or the rabbles which marched with banners which they seldom understood. But now he was one and part of them since he'd chosen a course emotionally. Caught in this crazy shaikhdom the Foreign Secretary hadn't counted. He'd pretended for a while, of course; he'd pretended his duty lay here, talking to Mortimer with an unaccustomed pomposity about accepting the responsibility which unexpectedly had been dropped on him. It had been a rare self-deception. Responsibility was one thing, a plain challenge quite another. Responsibility was for the Foreign Secretary but the challenge was Vincent Gale's. Very well then, he'd accepted it; he'd sat at desks for far too long, he'd considered and decided but as a man he'd done nothing. But now he'd put his banner up, tattered perhaps, and suspect of middle age. He'd carry it while they let him, though. As for the Foreign Secretary. . . .

He was someone who worked in London.

'A penny for your thoughts, my dear.'

'You'd have to pay more than that for them.'

She didn't press him and he accepted it; he said as a matter of simple fact: 'I'm afraid it's not a starter to put Ernest on the Council.'

'I can't truthfully say I thought it was.' She added smoothly: 'So you'll kill him instead.'

'No. I explained——'

With the first impatience of the day she said: 'So what's the difference? If you take him yourself he'll be hanged for murder, and if you let your friends withdraw him he'll be shot for having failed them.'

'You don't think he deserves quite that?'

'Deserves?' She shrugged again. 'You mustn't ask a woman to make judgements of morality. Or perhaps this is only a legal one—that's worse. All I know is that he'd do for us what will never get done while you British stand aside from it. Not that I don't see your point of view. You need the oil but by no means own it, so it's a political convenience that the only way to ship it is to bring it across a nominally independent state. So you let Ali draw his royalties and what happens inside the shaikhdom doesn't matter.'

'It's a pity you're not the shaikh,' he said.

'If you say that again I'll scream.'

Ernest had returned to the house of the man the Sikh had shot, belting back across the desert in a kind of exaltation. But it had died on him in a single night, its successor a black reaction. For he seemed to have miscalculated badly. It had seemed that the breaks had been coming at last, for the shaikh had gone and the results must be inevitable. The state across the border had claimed the shaikhdom for a decade and would in fact have grabbed by now if the British hadn't prevented it. It wasn't even necessary that an invasion should come at once since the British would see the danger and act first. They'd call in troops and Ernest knew what that meant: there'd be few to support them and an organized lobby to bay imperialism. One intervention bred another inexorably and the chaos which would follow would be the opportunity he'd waited for. This was the law and this the prophets. This was ineluctable.

And none of it had happened. The British had had a Minister killed, not the right one admittedly, but still a Minister of State. Their satellite shaikh had bolted shamelessly. . . .

And still they held off. They seemed astonishingly good at it.

At first Ernest had blamed his disappointment on the traditional cunning of capitalist statecraft. Vincent Gale would have some deep dark plan, something of almost mystical subtlety and wickedness. But this mood had been transient. Ernest had been taught that the laws of political conduct were universal and unchangeable, so that if Gale appeared to be defying them the reason could only be that there was some factor unknown to Ernest. And at once he had been uneasy since the only unknown factors must be those which he must answer for himself. He should have shot the shaikh and made quite sure. As it was Shaikh Ali might change his mind, or more likely he was parleying with his neighbour for some subordinate status but a guarantee of his income; he could even have flown to London and be re-negotiating his Treaty. Ernest frowned unhappily. If any of these happened it was his fault and his alone. He should have killed a man and hadn't, which could mean one thing and only one. It had happened to agents before him and would certainly happen again. He'd been away for far too long, he needed reconditioning.

His depression increased as he considered his need, for this question of absence from a familiar ideology bit deeper than the blunting of his edge. There was also the question of communication with his superiors, of the instructions which he so seldom saw. So seldom but not quite never, since when he'd been with his mistress he'd at least had a known address. At irregular intervals, a month perhaps, then two, a foreign seaman had sought him out. He hadn't valued the orders brought him, which had been vague, often no more than mere encouragement, but the simple sense of contact with his own and accustomed world. But in hiding he'd parted from even that; he was quite on his own and his drive was fading.

And instructions apart, it had occurred to him that the tradition of his profession, his own masters' especially, included the expedient of the spy-on-spy. It wouldn't be incredible if somewhere in the shaikhdom were a man who reported back on him. Ernest had considered it, for there had been times when any contact would have been welcome. But in the end he had thought it impossible. The circumstances were exceptional and the difficulties would be more so.

So that he was shaken by Luis' visit, even more shaken by the discovery that Luis wasn't his own spymaster but the agent of another Power. Luis had stated it immediately but he had brought with him a message. And he had been able to authenticate it.

He was a Spaniard, a technician at the Terminal, and he had walked in at midnight; he hadn't been armed but he'd been confident and businesslike, introducing himself formally. Ernest had asked him promptly: 'How did you find me?'

'A proper question, señor. I simply asked Stavridis. I've told you who I work for but I'm strictly a professional. I'll work for anyone who pays me so I've worked with Stavridis too. He wouldn't like that known, you know. Now that his own position is a good deal less than certain a connection with my humble self is the last thing he'd wish made public.' The Spaniard smiled with the irony of his race. 'Stavridis,' he said, 'will do most things to oblige me now—anything within reason. And giving me an address seemed reasonable.'

'And you've brought me a message?'

'Through my masters but from yours.'

'How do I know it's genuine?'

'There's nothing in writing, there wasn't time, but I'm prepared to recite you a couplet. I think it's a couplet though it's not in a language I know.'

'If you'd be good enough to do so, then.' Ernest knew about Spaniards—one couldn't be too polite to them.

Luis began to speak again and Ernest nodded. The accent was European but the words he could recognize, and not more than a dozen men would know them. Ernest said quietly: 'And now you will forget that, please.'

'Señor, I never knew it.'

'Good. Please give me your message.'

'You're to leave the shaikhdom immediately.' Luis held up his hand as Ernest began to question him. 'The order is clear and I'm sorry if it displeases you. There's a tanker which clears tomorrow and her flag you can guess. You're to sail with her, that's all.'

'Easier said than done, I think.'

'You're considering the difficulties—that she'll be sailing from the Terminal? But the details are all for me.' Luis felt in his pocket, handing Ernest a folded paper. 'That is a visitor's pass into the Terminal. You're to meet me at Gate C at ten o'clock. In European clothes, of course. Luggage is out. You're a friend of mine and I'll be treating you accordingly. I'll take you to the canteen and there we'll have a drink or two. Your pass will be examined as we go in, and because security is strict it will later be checked that you gave it up on exit. Since there won't be an exit you must leave that side to me.'

'With confidence.'

'I thank you.' Luis stood up; he bowed courteously but said with an unmistakable authority: 'Is that clear? At ten o'clock. Gate C.'

Ernest said dully: 'It's perfectly clear.'

The Spaniard bowed again and left.

Ernest sat on in the oil lamp's uncertain glow. He was tired but not frightened; he was simply without hope. There were matters for explanation here—why Luis who worked for one world should bring him orders from his own, even more why they should be withdrawing him when there was an outside chance of trouble still. But explanations weren't important when the motive at least was clear. They considered he'd failed so he'd failed in fact. Perhaps a better man was coming or perhaps. . . .

To Ernest it was irrelevant. This was sentence of death.

He looked at the pass and shrugged unsmiling. Very slowly he tore it to pieces.

The reply to Gale's telegram to the Prime Minister arrived at midnight. It had been sent *en clair* and Most Immediate, and Gale read it in astonishment. It was an unequivocal request for his immediate return and request put it much too mildly. There was still no news of any movement of troops across the border, but the shaikh's flight was in every newspaper and Questions had been put down to the Foreign Secretary. That he answer them was essential and Cabinet consultation was imperative. He should return at once.

Vincent Gale frowned. He'd given himself three days before the crunch, an increasing formalized pressure before the order. And he'd been wrong by two days and the half of another.

Well, one could make absurd mistakes. That was something he'd learnt in this hole of a shaikhdom.

He re-read the message and this time smiled. It occurred to him to tear it up, but the gesture would have had a melodrama which offended him. Instead he crumpled it lightly. He was wearing a dressing-gown and he put the cable in the pocket. Then he went back to bed.

Chapter Fourteen

Luis' message to the General had been delayed though not inordinately, for he was trusted and senior and had a system of communication with his masters which Ernest would have given his eyes for. It would have been inconceivable that he should contact the General directly, but even so the Colonel-General was reading the message six hours after Ernest had failed to keep his rendezvous at Gate C. He was displeased but not astonished. He was displeased because what had looked like an outstandingly successful operation had foundered on the indiscipline of a single man. And it *had* been successful, a small classic up to the point of failure. The General grunted. It had been four years at least since the last consignment of arms to what the stout man had called his oriental friends, more since the loaned technicians had been quietly recalled without replacement. But there was one thing they relied on still and it had been the General's conviction that they'd do most things to keep supplies of it. America wouldn't send it them and Europe wanted cash or gold. The stout man had agreed the plan and the machine had rolled efficiently. Ernest's masters had resented it, the breach had perceptibly widened, but the blackmail had worked and quickly. The Colonel-General smiled dourly. They worked fast when they'd once decided; he hated them but he gave them that. So the message had gone to Luis and the means to prove that it wasn't a fake.

. . . Most successful—almost copy-book. Except that this Ernest had sunk it. That was irritating and something more but it wasn't perhaps surprising. Ernst hadn't been home for a full three years, and it was a rule in the General's own organization that no working agent on an assignment of any importance should be left abroad for more than fourteen months, even with the excellent communications which he knew that Ernest lacked. Ernest had begun to slip, and when they'd once slipped they were worse than useless. The General's smile changed to thoughtful frown. He'd said that to the stout man once: Ernest might think, he might even feel, and an agent who felt was a hostage to fortune. He'd feel pity for the natives, he'd be emotionally entangled. . . .

He'd be dangerous. And discipline like courage was expendable, a wasting asset unless renewed. It would have taken the highest discipline to accept recall from total failure, for Ernest would know what recall would mean. He'd be lucky to die with dignity.

The General smoked seldom but now he lit a thin cheroot, inhaling it like a cigarette, coughing, then settling to think. His object was clear still but not the means to gain it. The essential was that this ridiculous shaikhdom shouldn't escalate into a major confrontation between reluctant major Powers, but on that front the omens were hopeful. There'd been no fighting on the frontier and the General nodded approvingly. He could imagine the pressures which the British would deploy against the clap-crippled, failing king. They were still competent politically when they forgot about the gunboats. And they hadn't fallen into the trap of calling in their own troops first. They'd left their Foreign Secretary in the shaikhdom. . . .

Yes, but there was the danger still, however smoothly the other hazards had been smothered. Charles Russell himself had recognized it, since apart from the professional humiliation of having one's Foreign Secretary murdered it would be something which no government could reasonably ignore. A junior Minister perhaps—they were putting out some story about a thief and stealing money—but hardly a Foreign Secretary on top of him. The British would have to act or be an international laughing-stock, and any action meant intervention.

Intervention could lead to appalling crisis. He'd recently seen it happen.

The General found his cheroot had gone out; he tapped the ash off and relit it unfussily. He saw the existing situation as an uncertain balance. Uncertain—that troubled him. On the one hand Ernest's chances of killing Gale were minimal, since Russell had reinforced his bodyguard and it would be unlikely in the extreme that Ernest could even get near him. But there were difficulties about arresting Ernest, Russell had taken them seriously, and the British would tread warily in any action which could start trouble in the bazaar. In the end no doubt they'd have to, but there'd be delay at least, and whilst Ernest was at large there was the outside chance that he'd somehow reach Vincent Gale. A desperate man with an automatic rifle. . . .

And motive, the Colonel-General thought—a burning motive. Not theory now, the knowledge that if Vincent Gale died violently the British would have to act, but the solid personal motive to redeem himself. For if the British were forced to intervene Ernest's mission would have succeeded. He needn't go home again, or not to face inquiry; he'd go home as a successful man, to fireworks perhaps and formal meals, to whatever passed for compliment in the barbarous land he came from. He had one chance in fifty of killing Gale but a multiplied motive to try to.

The General walked to the window, for a moment staring

147

out of it. . . . Motive, he thought for the second time: it was invariably decisive. He'd have to be quite certain so he'd have to accept the risks.

Back at his desk he wrote a second order to Luis. It had occurred to him to consult Charles Russell—Russell had insisted that the Executive could handle its own erasements. But Luis would know where Ernest was and it wasn't a certainty that the Executive had him pinned yet. He could tell them of course, but it would all take time, and time was of the essence. Besides, there would be explanations and the General detested them. He hadn't told Russell that he'd an agent of his own in the shaikhdom: that would have been an impertinence, and he hadn't flown to London to offend a *cher collègue*. The General's smile returned, not dour. He was shooting another man's bear at that, and in those regrettable circumstances it was wiser to shoot, make apologies later.

He'd apologize very handsomely but he'd determined he'd play this one safe. He was a Russian and proud of it, and he sent his second order without a qualm.

Ernest was lying on his string cot, awake in the small hours. He was sleeping little or not at all; he was sick but not physically and he wished that he were. If he'd had a fever he could at least expect its crisis, and then he could sleep at last. Instead he was sick mentally, but not so sick that he didn't know his malady. The apparatus of self-criticism was functioning remorselessly. If he could only sleep. . . .

It was useless, he decided, it was better to face the facts. The first was his failure but that was self-evident; what tortured him was the knowledge that he'd brought it upon himself. These feckless feeble people should have been instruments of policy, not men and women whose misery wrung his bowels. What were they good for? Nothing. It had been a pipe dream to suppose that any riot he could have organized would have ended in seizing an armoury. At best there would have been some pointless disorder, the looting of Sindhi *bhaiband* shops, the burning of booths of Marwari moneylenders. Of course that was well worth doing—Marwaris were the cruellest extortioners of all—but it wouldn't be revolution nor even within a mile of it. And the man he had almost trusted, the desert Arab, had died for nothing. His widow was getting restless, too, since Ernest's continued presence was a continuing threat to her. Only Arab hospitality, the inescapable obligation of her husband's invitation, made it unthinkable to suggest his leaving. It would have been unheard of, a total breach of a mandatory code. Ernest felt sorry for her, embarrassed that he was obliged to impose himself.

He put his hands behind his head. This was very wrong thinking and a symptom of his sickness, but it was nothing against his flat disobedience of orders. He'd been ordered to return and he had not. It was partly that he hadn't dared but he knew there was other motive. Somewhere there was another world. . . . He was astonished to discover that he was thinking of his parents. He could hardly remember them. His father, a big blond friendly man, his mother who sometimes spoke English to him. They were figures in a shadowplay but they weren't without significance; they'd given him life and genes which were immutable. Heredity or training, then—he'd been taught to back conditioning. Very well, that was right still—he needed reconditioning. It was a word for machinery but he'd been trained as a machine.

Not, he thought unhappily, that these reflections had any value to him. What was pressing immediately was the fact that he was in hiding, and in a room which was the perfect trap. There was one way in, a ladder, and no other way out. It had been a store room once, a granary, and where a bedroom might have had a window there was a pair of wooden doors. Ernest had left them open in the grim night heat, and above the square of starlight he could make out the ancient hoist, a crumbling beam with a rusted pulley at its extremity. But he hadn't a rope and it wasn't important. If they came for him, *when* they came for him, they'd leave a man outside the house, and dangling on a rope he'd be a sitter.

A sitter—it was the proper word. For Ernest had decided that they wouldn't trouble to arrest him. Why indeed should they? He'd killed a British Minister and that would mean a formal trial. They wouldn't want a formal trial. He wouldn't decide for a trial himself so therefore they wouldn't either. Publicity, the newspapers, a nine days' wonder. . . . That wasn't the way he'd been taught to think and it was unlikely the British were stupider. No, an armed man or men would come up the ladder, then. . . .

Well, he still had the rifle. And it couldn't be long—not now. Stavridis knew his hideout and they'd twist Stavridis easily. He looked round the tiny room again. He was a rat in a hole and felt it.

His nerves, stretched to breaking, tautened again intolerably at the creak of the ladder. He reached for the rifle, swinging his legs from the unsteady cot, covering the door. A creak again and a voice he thought he recognized.

'Señor Ernest?' it said.

He didn't answer.

'Señor Ernest? It is I. It is Luis.'

'I'm not coming with you. I can't.'

'Señor, it isn't that. I've news.'

Ernest stood up. He still held the rifle and he walked to the door. At it he said briefly: 'Tell.'

'This time it's written orders.'

Ernest unlocked the padlock. The chain went through a staple and he freed it. He had meant to do it silently, then stand back with the rifle, but the chain was old and rusty and it squeaked in the staple shrilly. The door burst inwards violently and Luis was on top of him. A knife he had and he knew how to use it. Ernest was holding the rifle still but they were much too close to fire it. Luis' thrust was half-way home by now but Earnest smashed the rifle down. It blocked part of the upswing but not the whole. Ernest grunted at a stomach wound, then brought his butt up sharply. He was fighting by instinct, trying to break the close-in brawl, somehow to fire the rifle. He could use a knife and could use a gun, but gun against knife in a chest-to-chest *mêlée*. . . .

With something like astonishment he saw that he'd been lucky. The butt had smashed the Spaniard's chin and by reflex he'd broken contact. He was staggering still and Ernest had him. The rifle was on his hip, his finger moving . . .

He checked it incredulous, staring. Luis was on his feet but only just—only the limitless courage of the Spaniard held him upright. His eyes were glazing, his legs quite gone. To fire would wake the neighbourhood and clearly it wasn't necessary. Luis, at last, had dropped the knife. He crashed blindly against a wooden wall, somehow came off it standing. Ernest had picked the knife up but Luis was coming back at him. He was less than half-conscious and now barehanded, and Ernest with a real regret gutted him scientifically. Luis began to spin again. He reeled across the little room, bent double but always silent. At the door of the loading-port he shied instinctively, then his legs collapsed finally. He disappeared. Ernest counted three before the noise.

. . . No need for Stavridis to blow me now. They'll find the body and that's enough.

Ernest went back to his uncomfortable cot, examining his wound. He'd been lucky again but not that lucky. Luis hadn't cut his stomach-wall so his intestines were in one piece still, but he'd an eight-inch flesh wound and he was bleeding from it strongly. Ernest looked at his stomach grimly for this was doctor's work for certain. Stitches and lots of them. He rummaged in his suitcase for a single piece of plaster. . . . Useless. He hadn't a sheet but he tore an old shirt up.

Hopeless again. He was losing blood fast and would go on losing it.

He lay down on the cot again, trying not to watch his wound. There were worse ways to die than quietly bleeding to death.

They'd sometimes made him watch them.

Chapter Fifteen

Robert Mortimer's daily report by telegram was normally the first paper Russell read when he arrived at the Executive, but this one had been thought sufficiently important to be sent to his flat and he was considering it with his morning tea. His first emotion had been anger—the General had made a fool of him; he'd never intended that Ernest should be discreetly withdrawn from the shaikhdom: instead he'd meant to kill him from the start. That, after all, was in the tradition of his formidable organization—the simple, final sanction and remorselessly applied. Russell had snorted crossly but had recovered his good humour as thought replaced reflex. For why should the General lie to him, and why fly to London, talking co-operation, if the predetermined object had been as simple as killing Ernest? It was much more likely that the General's intention had been precisely as he had proposed it but that his superiors had jibbed. He'd insisted that he must ask them and his masters had turned it down. Which of course had put the General to some embarrassment. He could hardly leak to Russell about a political decision at the highest level —he couldn't, that is, and expect to live—and if the further decision had been to liquidate Ernest instead of blackmailing his employers to withdraw him, then equally the General could hardly write blandly to Russell that he was now proposing to poach on Russell's land. That would have been an insult—worse than the act of poaching. Charles Russell nodded tolerantly; he'd have chosen the lesser evil too.

Not, he thought now, that it very much mattered. The General's superiors had decided on killing Ernest, so the General himself had issued orders to do so. And something had clearly gone wrong with them. According to Mortimer's telegram there was the body of a Spaniard in the street out side Ernest's house. Untidy—very. The Spaniard had been working in the Terminal and Mortimer was checking on his background. But that again wasn't immediately important. What was immediate were two guesses and a fact, and if the guesses were indeed as reasonable as they seemed to be, the deduction which must be made from them. Russell began to scribble on the back of Mortimer's telegram:

1. My enchanting chum the General had his original plan turned down.
2. He was told to kill Ernest and subsequently tried to.
3. There's a stiff in the street outside Ernest's house, so the presumption at least is that Ernest's alive inside it.
4. *Which puts the ball firmly back with me.*

Russell finished his tea reflectively, then telephoned to the Prime Minister, smiling, thinking of royalty. For he had one thing in common with these agreeable anachronisms: he couldn't leave the country without the Prime Minister's permission. There was the briefest of conversations and the consent he had expected, then he turned to a timetable. There was a flight which would land him in the shaikhdom next morning, even allowing for the orthodox three or four hours' delay, and now he telephoned to the Executive. It was hardly worth going there, and moreover he wanted to think. They were to book him and confirm it, and to signal to Major Mortimer the moment the seat was firm.

He walked early next morning into a heat already intolerable. He was wearing a silk suit and an ancient Bombay bowler. Both were elegant but old-fashioned; for more years ago than he cared to think about Russell had seen service in India. He hadn't enjoyed the East at all. It had put him in his place perhaps, but that place had been the West and he'd been glad of it.

Colonel Charles Russell was an unrepentant European.

He drove with Robert Mortimer to Bolton's bungalow. Bolton and Gale were awaiting them, sitting on the veranda under a creaking but still serviceable fan. Russell and Mortimer took the two empty chairs and Gale began laconically.

'I won't bother you with the political background. We'll talk about that later if we must.' It had occurred to him to add: 'And if I'm still in a position to,' but he'd decided it would be premature. He was still formally Foreign Secretary. He turned to Russell as the senior. 'So regarding it as police work . . . ?'

'Regarding it as police work it's a beast.' Charles Russell looked at Mortimer. 'Any background on this Spaniard yet?'

'No sir, not yet. One little thing, though. The knife in his belly was Spanish-made.'

'Implying that Ernest turned it against him? Implying that if he did so he's most likely alive himself?'

Robert Mortimer nodded.

'Any means of confirming it?'

'None short of looking, sir. We've recovered the Spaniard's body but that's our limit peacefully.'

'Ay, there's the rub.' Russell switched smoothly to Bolton. 'I've been briefed about your difficulties in risking any action in the bazaar. I realize them and sympathize but it looks like this Spaniard's forced us.'

Bolton said carefully: 'You sent men of your own here and I gathered we could use them.'

'Most certainly if you think they'd help.'

'They'd minimize the risks but not avoid them.'

'I see.' Russell returned to Vincent Gale; he said with the

155

detachment of the very senior official: 'So that's how it looks to policemen. It's not ultimately our decision, though.'

'I'd be happy to leave it.'

'I can't accept.'

The Foreign Secretary reflected. 'May I put you in the box?' he asked.

'I've been there before but only once. That was in a traffic case.'

'Then this Ernest tried to murder me?'

'Almost but not quite certainly.'

'And he did kill poor Heldon?'

'He did.'

'And now somebody's tried to clean him up—to shut his mouth my guess would be, but I don't think the motive's essential.' For an instant Gale hesitated. 'I take it it wasn't you?' he asked.

'It was not,' Russell said. But he didn't sound offended.

'You'll forgive me the question. I dare say you'd plan to kill a man but I'm certain you wouldn't botch it.'

Charles Russell bowed.

'So we've an attempted killing and two people killed. One of them was a Minister, the other, it seems, was a second intending killer. Plus the original killer free still.'

'That states it brutally. Also with accuracy.'

'Then we'll have to take the risks. I think. We'll have to go and get him, even armed.'

There was a second of silence and the faintest sigh. Bolton rose, bringing drinks. Mortimer produced a street plan, spreading it on the table, marking it in pencil for Russell's benefit. The three men talked quietly, professionals engaged at their profession. Gale didn't interrupt them. He'd decided and he was out of it, just a man who made decisions.

It was other men's risks again.

The princess was trying to make sense of the weeping woman. She was the cousin of one of her servants—that much was clear since the servant had fearfully brought her— but she was telling her story in gasps and groans, with the exaggerated tragedy of the Orient. Madame was feeling extremely French, but she was an Arab too with an Arab's patience, and slowly the story formed itself into a certain grim lucidity. This woman had a sister and she'd married a desert Arab since she'd come from the desert herself. He'd arrived on the Coast in search of work and he hadn't been doing badly. He'd had a job at the hotel and had bought an old house where they all lived together. Yes, he hadn't been doing badly till he'd met this accursed foreigner. The foreigner had ruined him. . . . What sort of foreigner? But the woman wasn't sure of that. He spoke Arabic better than she did but he looked like a European. There was a rumour that he had yellow blood but if that was true it showed hardly at all. The woman had started to weep again and Madame had silently let her. 'And so?' she asked finally.

So on the evening they'd opened the Council this foreigner had gone out on some devil's work. He had taken her sister's husband, too, he had him in some wicked spell, and the man had been shot by an infidel Sikh.

. . . And then?

And then—ah, Allah's mercy. The foreigner had come back to her sister's house. She was a widow now, but he'd come there first on her husband's invitation. He was a guest. It was unthinkable to ask him to leave, and in any case they were terrified of him. The house was watched, they could see the watcher. And last night there had been a dreadful fight. A man had arrived, another foreigner, and in the morning his body had been lying in the street outside. Three Englishmen had come and quietly taken it. No Sikhs yet— that horror would follow later. The foreigner's door was locked and he wouldn't answer. And the foreigner had a rifle.

The woman had fumbled in her voluminous and not scrupulously clean clothing. She produced a crumpled paper which she handed to the princess.

'What's this?'

'It's a letter.'

'I can see. But where did it come from?'

The woman hung her head. 'My sister—my sister found it. She can't read it and nor can I, but we showed it to an uncle. He says it's in English but it's signed by Shaikh Ali. My sister said to bring it you.'

Madame held her hand out.

To whomsoever it may concern

I, Ali bin Hasan bin Ibrahim, commend to your duty the bearer of this certificate, Ernest or Ernst, my servant. He who may oblige him obliges also myself and may address himself accordingly for the discharge of the obligation.

The princess said gently: 'Your sister took this from the foreign man?'

'I . . . yes.'

'You did very well to bring it me. Now bring me the foreigner.'

'Your Highness, how can I?'

'Simply.' The princess rang a bell imperiously. 'I'll send you in my car and it will fly my own flag. No man will stop it but I'll give you an escort too.' She gave brief orders to the major-domo. 'And that within the hour,' she said. She looked back at the trembling woman. 'Sit.'

'Your Highness——'

'Sit.'

The woman squatted on the floor and a Louis-Seize clock ticked cosily. Presently she said softly: 'Your Highness . . .' Her voice tailed away.

'Yes?'

'I'm a presumptuous nothing, your servant, I——'

'Speak, sister. Freely.'

For the first time the woman raised eyes from the ground.

'You're taking a terrible risk,' she said. They were two women talking.

'I know I am.'

'But why?'

Madame picked the letter up, reading it, translating. It wasn't difficult since Ali had thought in Arabic. '"I commend to your duty. . . ." '

The princess smiled. 'He charges us,' she said. 'You see?'

The woman nodded quickly once; she said simply: 'Of course.'

It was three in the afternoon when Charles Russell looked down from the veranda at the almost completed preparations. The heat was appalling but the hour had been chosen deliberately. Most people slept in it, and any possible mitigation of the dangers of a raid into the bazaar was welcome. Russell walked to the railing. There was one of the armoured cars which Bolton hid discreetly for occasions of genuine urgency, two jeeps and a large saloon. There wasn't a Sikh in sound or sight. Bolton would drive the A.F.V. with two of Russell's men in it, and Mortimer and a third would travel in the jeep. The last two, reserves, would go in the large saloon. It was Russell's intention to add himself unobtrusively, but it was something he hadn't mentioned. There would be protest and fuss and he hated both; it wasn't quite impossible that Gale would flatly forbid him. So he had held his peace and was holding it still as he looked along the veranda. At the other end of it the five visitors from the Executive were drinking lemonade. They were solid-looking men, but ill at ease in shorts and tropical headgear. Hard hats and rolled umbrellas were their working dress, for in the Security Executive the upper stratum of strongarms affected the habit of prosperous solicitors. No macintoshes—ever. But now they had their coats off and all were sweating freely. Mortimer was briefing them finally.

They were comfortable-looking men and Russell drew

comfort from them. But not placidity. He was conscious indeed of an ancient thrill. . . . Battle—the hour before it. The Divisional General would be briefing his commanders, giving his final pep talk with a confidence which in any other circumstances would be insulting. He'd be describing enemy dispositions as though he'd inspected them personally, then he'd add the ritual saver that no doubt there would be casualties, but with the sort of troops which you gentlemen have the honour to command . . .

Charles Russell sighed, then chuckled grimly. For of course it cut both ways. Sometimes you walked into utter hell—Intelligence had been wrong. And sometimes the enemy had quietly gone: all you met was a rearguard. Intelligence had ballsed again.

There had once been a proposal to rename the Security Executive the Department of Special Intelligence. Russell had promptly threatened to resign.

Gale came out from the bungalow, watching the final touches. Two European mechanics were checking the engines of the jeep and the big saloon, and Bolton in the armoured car was making short dashes, then banging his foot down savagely. He seemed to attach importance to his brakes. At last he was satisfied. He walked back to the veranda and Russell's five men stood up. Gale said compulsively: 'That bloody bazaar—I don't much like it.'

'No more do I.'

The landing at the ladder-head was small and too cramped to work on, and it took the two men some time to force the door. Ernest lay on his cot whilst they did so. He still had the rifle but not the will to use it; he was sick and tired of killing and moreover barely conscious. They had to carry him to the car and to Madame's, and they put him on the sofa in her room. They had let him bring the rifle since he'd managed to threaten to fight for it, and the princess's orders had been to avoid above all things a disturbance in the native town.

She looked at him once, then gave crisp, precise orders. . . .
Water and disinfectant; bandages and brandy; and send the
car for her personal doctor. The brandy was perhaps a risk
but she decided she'd have to take it. She neatly made him
swallow some, watching him come round slowly. He looked
at the civilized beautiful room and he looked at its evident
owner. At last he asked weakly: 'Where am I?'

'I can't say with friends but you can take it I'm your
hostess.'

She could see he didn't follow but it didn't at all distress her.
She'd been honest and that mattered most, she hadn't started
him with a lie. She went on quietly: 'They tell me you've
a stomach wound and I can see you're losing blood still.' The
opulent sofa had quickly stained but if Madame had noticed
she ignored it. 'I've sent for my doctor. He's not exactly
Harley Street but he's worked in France and he's clean and
safe. Meanwhile I'm going to wash your wound.'

He protested feebly but she began to undress him, catching her breath but unflinching. The wound didn't look septic
and in the climate of the shaikhdom that was lucky. But he'd
lost far too much blood for safety. 'I'm going to hurt you,'
she said, 'but you needn't fear. I once did a little nursing.'
She cleaned the wound and dressed it lightly. Ernest grimaced
but he didn't utter. When the doctor arrived she left
them.

It was nearly an hour before he returned to her. Like the
manager of the hotel he was a Christian Lebanese and he
spoke in fair French. 'I've stitched him,' he said, 'but he
shouldn't be moved.'

'I didn't intend to.'

The doctor was silent. These were an Arab lady's quarters,
his own admission to them a considerable concession to
modernity. He waited for Madame to speak again.

'You say he shouldn't be moved?' she asked.

'Not far, if at all.'

'Could we take him to another room?'

'I gave him an anaesthetic but he's almost come through it now. Have you a stretcher?'

She shook her head. 'But we could take down a door.'

The doctor said with an evident doubt: 'But carefully. . . . And he'd need constant nursing.'

'I once took a course in it.'

'Then I'll call again this evening—for the moment I've done everything.' The doctor bowed and took his leave. He wasn't paid to talk of hospitals, far less to ask questions.

The Princess Nahid went back to her room, sitting down quietly, waiting for Ernest to recover consciousness. Two of her ladies sat with her. When Ernest stirred she went to him. He opened his eyes, made an effort to focus, but she waited till he was ready. At last he said faintly: 'I know who you are . . . I think I do.'

'It isn't important.'

'To me it is.'

'Listen,' she said, 'we'll have to move you. You're a man, you see, and only a special sort of man can sleep in this part of the house. I know you're not one of them.'

She saw again that he hadn't followed, so she said again firmly: 'I'm sorry I'll have to move you, but there's a room in the stables and it isn't uncomfortable. It's my guest room really, and you're a guest.'

'My rifle,' he said.

She'd forgotten about the rifle. It had been stood in a corner, as alien in a boudoir as a sewing box in a public bar.

'You won't need that.'

'I do, I must. I . . .' She saw he had nearly gone again, but for a moment he rallied.

'I don't receive armed guests,' she said.

'Guest—I'm a guest?'

'Of course.'

'But why?'

'You wouldn't understand at all.'

She waited till he slept again, then they carried him carefully out, down the long cloister into the block which Gale had recognized as store rooms and stables. The windows, as he had guessed, faced away from the courtyard, and at the end of a corridor a room had been made habitable. There was even a bath which worked. The Princess Nahid made Ernest comfortable, then returned to her splendid room.

She went at once to the rifle, handling it with confidence, stripping it expertly—stock, barrel and bolt, and magazine. She'd been properly taught with firearms and she looked at the barrel a second time. . . . Not that fatal one up the spout still. Then she locked the four pieces in a drawer of her writing desk.

She sent for her car with urgency.

The procession had formed and was moving slowly—the armoured car leading, the jeep, then the big saloon. Charles Russell was in it but only just, for there'd been the protests he'd feared and they'd made him argue. He had in fact delayed them half an hour.

They had started to move when the armoured car stopped suddenly. They were half-way across the baked-earth compound when another car came into it. It was driving fast in a cloud of dust, and the dust increased as the tourer braked. When it subsided a woman was coming out of it. She ran lithely up the wooden steps, and Russell in the big saloon permitted himself a whistle. He climbed out too and walked back on to the veranda.

The Foreign Secretary was facing the Princess Nahid. He seemed to be speechless, and that, Russell thought, was interesting. Politicians had their weaknesses but they could usually find the word for it. Madame turned to him easily. 'You're Colonel Charles Russell, I think,' she said. 'We've met before in London.'

'I hadn't forgotten.' He bowed politely but spoke with sincerity.

The courtesies were interrupted by the Foreign Secretary; he was saying incredulously: 'The princess says that Ernest is at her house. And he's wounded as well as armed.'

'He went there?'

'No, she took him.'

'Indeed? But wouldn't we all be happier sitting down?' Russell pulled a chair up for Madame, then walked again to the railing; he called clearly but short of shouting: 'Major Mortimer!'

'Sir?'

'Ask Chief Superintendent Bolton to have the goodness to hold the party.'

'Sir.'

Russell returned with another chair. Madame was sitting already but Vincent Gale still stood. He said quietly: 'I don't believe it.'

'I'd say myself I can hardly believe it.' Charles Russell spoke with a faint reproof. Mr. Vincent Gale was under evident strain but one didn't call ladies liars.

'It's perfectly true,' the princess said.

'Of course it is. But if I may ask your motive——?'

'You wouldn't understand it.'

'I might try.'

Madame considered. 'He had a letter from my brother.'

'A letter to you?'

'Not exactly. It was a letter to all and sundry but I'm Ali's own sister.'

'A letter of recommendation?'

'Yes, and more.'

Russell said astonishingly: 'Then I understand perfectly.' He rose with decision. 'May I take you to your car, then?'

She looked down into the compound, at the armoured car and the silent men. 'You won't come to my house and start shooting it out? Men fighting all over a woman's house. . . .'

'I assure you I never considered it.'

Mr. Vincent Gale made the faintest sound but neither even looked at him.

'Then you may see me to my car,' she said.

They walked down from the veranda and Russell held the door open. As she climbed in the princess said softly: 'He isn't armed now. He was—a rifle. But I took it away and hid it.'

'You did that?' Charles Russell thought it over, saying at last: 'If you'll forgive me the impertinence may I ask if you've ever married?'

She shook her head, smiling.

'Then I venture to commend myself.'

She began to laugh and he took her hand and kissed it. As the car began to move she said: 'And what'll you do now, *mon cher*?'

'We'll talk and we'll talk, and all, I expect, quite uselessly.'

'Men are great ones for talking.'

'And women do dreadfully foolish things.'

'I don't think this was foolish. Inconvenient, certainly. That's true for me too. I don't have to house a criminal. And yet I do. We impossible Arabs with our ideas about obligation. Our antiquated ideas. . . .'

'I'm getting antique myself,' he said.

Chapter Sixteen

Charles Russell had suggested that they sleep on it, though his own mind was clear on the only course possible. What he feared was a phenomenon which he'd often observed before: men unaccustomed to violence, outside its normal ambit, could react with embarrassing violence when unexpectedly exposed to it. So it wasn't quite impossible that Gale would now give orders which Russell would regret at once and Gale would regret at leisure, such, for instance, as taking an armed party to the house of the Princess Nahid and there arresting Ernest at gunpoint. Gale had been thrown into a world which would be strange to him, and Russell knew that judgement was a reflex to circumstance at least as much as logic. He'd proposed that they all think quietly and he'd slid away from protest.

So they met early next morning under punkahs already turning. Gale said at once: 'We'll take the princess first, I think. Why do you think she did it?' He spoke with a hint of injury and clearly he hadn't slept well.

It was the question which Russell had feared the most— God damn and blast all lawyers. He hadn't an answer, or not to Gale. The Princess Nahid was an upper-crust Arab, and to Russell that was final. He hid a tolerant smile. This revulsion from sensible and self-regarding action, from the values of the market place—only Arabs and Spaniards had it still, and perhaps an Anglo-Irishman. Like Russell himself who had understood instinctively. But Gale was an Englishman, lawyer and politician. Russell said urbanely: 'Madame is a woman.' It sounded distinctly shallow but that didn't worry him. It was never his practice to appear to be over-clever.

'If you're hinting quite improperly——'

Vincent Gale had sounded angry but Russell was blander than ever. 'We could take all this too seriously. Whatever her motive and I'm guessing at that—' he crossed schoolboy but expiatory fingers—'the fact remains that she took him in. But he's pretty severely wounded and she's disarmed him.' Russell turned to Mortimer. They hadn't rehearsed it but their understanding was excellent. Mortimer said crisply: 'That's the situation as we face it.'

'Quite.' Russell looked at Gale again but his expression told him nothing. Gale was in fact remembering that in effect he'd been overridden. Madame had arrived the day before, the goddess, he thought sourly, in that ancient machine, and within the limits of bare good manners she'd ignored him; instead she'd turned instinctively to Russell. Gale had made no decisions since he hadn't been asked to do so. And very probably rightly. He was good at decisions, but they were decisions of a certain kind. Give him the papers, some competent minuting by well-briefed subordinates, and he was as likely as the next man to bring the penny down right. But put on the table some senseless act, something blankly incomprehensible to the administrative mind, and it was the Russells people turned to. He asked at last: 'So what do we do now?'

'I could go and talk to Ernest,' Russell said.

'But what can you offer him?'

Charles Russell sighed inaudibly. It was the classic fallacy that men acted reasonably when they stared at a final crisis, that they'd balance a profit against a loss, that they'd be logical in extremity. He said softly: 'Almost nothing.'

'We might offer him a trial in a British court. For what that's worth to him.'

'I'd say not very much. The story we've fancied so far is that he killed a foreigner in a bedroom in the course of committing a theft. That's still capital murder.'

'We can't possibly live with that one if it goes to an English judge. Down the Coast—well, perhaps. But never in London.'

'You're now suggesting we tell the truth? That Ernest was really after you but killed Heldon by mistake?'

'I never liked the other.'

No, Russell thought, but he'd never been asked expressly; he'd raised an eyebrow at innuendo but he'd silently let it pass. Vincent Gale was a lawyer. Russell said firmly: 'Then it's a lifer in a foreign jail.'

'You're not being very helpful.' The Foreign Secretary spoke with a pique he seldom allowed himself. He looked tired and was feeling it.

Russell answered him impassively; he might almost have been talking to himself. 'Not so many years ago there was a spate of state trials in Russia. Day after day the old guard stood up, men with a lifetime in communism. They all confessed to most dreadful crimes—they were traitors, spies, or secretly fascist beasts. And why do you think they did it? Some mysterious drug which we've never discovered? Straight torture?' Charles Russell shook his head. 'There was maltreatment no doubt, the witholding of sleep, a brutal softening-up in fact. But I don't think that was all of it. When your life is cut off at a single stroke, everything you've worked for——'

'You go willingly to the stake, you think? You make the final act of witness?' Vincent Gale sounded sceptical; he said disapprovingly: 'But I've never met a martyr.'

'Haven't you? But that wasn't quite my point, you know.

I'm no sort of psychiatrist, I wasn't trying to be subtle. All I was recording was an observed and observable fact: devoted men, men wholly committed, can behave unpredictably when the solid ground they've trodden for half a life-time . . .' Charles Russell hesitated; he knew he was right but he doubted that he was communicating; he said at last: 'When they come to the end of the road.'

'You're talking of communists?'

'The best sort of communist.'

'Of whom Ernest is one?'

'Of course.'

There was a formidable silence before Gale spoke again; he said in his special courtroom voice: 'Then you're pro-posing a talk with Ernest? To see, in effect, what develops or doesn't.'

'It wouldn't commit us, it would leave us free later. And I like to meet my enemies. If I could speak to Ernest——'

'Then I'll go myself.' Vincent Gale hadn't hesitated.

'But——'

'I'm still the princess's friend, you know.'

'But not, I think, Ernest's.'

'Are you?'

'In a way,' Russell said.

The drive to the princess's house had given Gale time to think and he had used it. This should be just a social call—that was the way to handle it. He'd be calling on Madame but he'd be grateful too for a word with Ernest. He wouldn't commit himself, or not prematurely; he'd call and she'd make the running.

He was shown to her splendid room again and she rose gracefully in greeting. She seemed pleased enough to see him but she didn't conceal surprise. 'It was Charles Russell I was expecting,' she said frankly.

It flicked his pride but he hid the wound. 'I thought I'd better come myself.'

'You'll have come to see my guest, not me. I was expecting that but I'm not too sure. He seems a little stronger but the doctor isn't happy yet.'

He wasn't, she thought—he was worried grey. And not about his surgery.

She considered, then shrugged, leading Gale down the corridor to the door of the stable block. 'I oughtn't to come too, you know, or not without other women. In any case you'll want to talk. Alone, I imagine.' Her smile was social, the words were barbed. 'Go straight along the corridor till ·you come to a sort of hall. There's a good deal of rubbish so mind your step. Also a guest room. There are three or four doors but the guest room's the newly-painted one.'

'It's really very kind of you.'

She stayed silent at the irony but opened the cloister door. Vincent Gale went through it and she shut it behind him quietly. Then she went back to her room.

She began to make coffee, frowning in irritation. She had expected Charles Russell and would have trusted him entirely, for instinct assured her warmly they had a language much in common. But Vincent Gale. . . . She shrugged again. In a sense he had offended her. Under the politician's practised ease was a personal uncertainty, and men who weren't sure of manhood did things and accepted risks which no man accepted who was certain he wasn't a coward. Not that there was the slightest risk in talking to an unarmed invalid. She glanced at the writing desk, remembering Ernest's rifle. Then she stared at it hard again. A little shakily she walked to it.

The scratches were hardly visible but the drawer slid open without unlocking. The rifle had gone.

For a second she didn't credit it. . . . A stomach wound in stitches still, and God knew how much blood lost. . . . She put a hand on the writing desk, steadying herself, then ran down the cloister, not Madame now but a frightened woman.

170

She opened the connecting door and for a moment the half dark blinded her. At the end of the corridor Vincent Gale was sitting on a broken packing case. He was smoking a cigarette but rose at once; he said a little formally, muting a faint apology: 'I was considering what line I'd take.'

If she noticed his manner she didn't care; she said panting: 'He's got a gun.'

Gale didn't answer.

'He's got back the rifle.'

'I heard you the first time.'

'You don't understand. He had a rifle when he came here but I took it away and locked it up. Somehow he's got it back again. God knows. . . .' She was breathless, not thinking. 'He's tough,' she said.

Vincent Gale looked at her. His expression had changed to a frigid rage. 'Have you another gun?' he asked.

She shook her head.

'Perhaps it's just as well at that. I'm not used to fire-arms.'

'Vincent, I think he's gone over the hill, a case, you know, a breakdown. So does the doctor.' She pulled herself together. 'With a rifle——'

'I'm still going to see your guest,' he said.

'But you can't—you can't possibly. He's an armed man and dangerous. Charles Russell——'

'Damn Colonel Charles Russell and all his men.' He smiled at her unexpectedly. 'And now if you'd kindly go away.'

'But Vincent——'

'Be off.'

'But——'

He took her by the shoulders, turning her away from him, pushing her firmly down the corridor to the door she'd left open. Without change of pace he had her through it. He was stronger than she had thought he was. He shut the door, then went back to his packing case.

The Princess Nahid walked unsteadily up the cloister. She telephoned Bolton's bungalow and there caught Charles Russell. He listened, swore softly, then told her to do nothing. He was coming himself. At once.

The princess sat down. She hadn't cried since childhood but now she sat down and wept.

Vincent Gale sat down too on the uncomfortable broken crate. His surroundings hadn't surprised him, for this was indeed the stable block he'd recognized originally. There were the muddle of ancient rubbish of which Madame had warned him, the accretion of centuries, and somewhere beyond another wall the soft stirring of animals. Only the smell was alien, the sour stink of camel dung. That and the freshly-painted door.

He stared at it uncertainly. It had been true that he'd been considering what line to take with Ernest, but he'd also been considering that door. Behind it he'd now find Ernest armed, but he hadn't thought only of Ernest. A guest room, she'd called it, and guest rooms meant guests. Discreetly sited and to Vincent Gale disturbing. He wasn't a conceited man and in most things a rigid realist, but there were matters where illusions weren't so much luxuries as negative but necessary props. And when a freshly-painted bedroom door had stripped them away remorselessly. . . .

He lit another cigarette. Whoever had used that room before, it was now used by Ernest. Behind that door was a sick man armed, a man who had tried to kill him. And there was so much to do still. This preposterous shaikhdom. For his visit had cleared his mind—the Foreign Secretary's. The oil must be kept but it wouldn't be kept like this. Messing about under a mystifying Arabian carpet intricately patterned with ancient treaties of protection, historical obligations to archaic shaikhs. It wouldn't do, it really wouldn't. The whole set-up was a powder barrel. The mystique of the old Coast hands, the Walter Woodards, the courteous obduracy of his

Permanent Under Secretary, the Englishman's fatal weakness for a feudal Arab in fancy dress. . . .

The fuse was alight and almost gone. You might keep the oil since its owners couldn't drink it. But not like this, not by some comic Council. A desperate heave into modern times—he could do it or he'd try to.

But not if a stranger shot him.

He began to think practically—sensibly, he told himself. He needn't have come to Madame's at all, thrusting himself into business for professionals. Ernest could be immobilized, Russell could picket the house, and though that solved nothing finally it would give them all time to think. He hadn't a valid reason to be sticking his amateur neck out. He had plans for this shaikhdom and to force them through he'd have to live.

He'd have to live, certainly, but he must live with himself as well. You couldn't push a woman through a door, then rejoin her nothing done. You couldn't if you still wanted her. The Foreign Secretary smiled wryly. He'd been thinking he'd sat at desks too long, deciding the risks of other men. It had been second-hand thinking, like going to a play, he knew, and with all of a bad play's failure to involve him. But this wasn't a play, it was Ernest armed. It was true he was weak still, the doctor wasn't happy yet. . . .

Ernest still had a rifle.

Mr. Vincent Gale rose slowly. This was reality, the phenomenal life he moved in, not his thoughts. And it had suddenly become extremely dangerous.

. . . Well, I asked for it.

He walked firmly to the painted door and threw it open. He was looking at Ernest down an automatic rifle. Ernest was propped on pillows and his face twitched paranoically. The gun wavered slightly but not off target. Ernest said weakly in a voice near to breaking: 'Please go away. I beg you. *Please*.'

. . . So this was what a doctor meant when he said that he wasn't quite happy.

'I only wanted a word or two. I'm Vincent Gale.'

'I know.'

Gale began to talk quietly but watching the rifle. He wasn't too certain that Ernest was understanding him. Once his head dropped alarmingly and Vincent Gale edged forward. Ernest forced himself back to consciousness. 'I'll shoot you,' he said absurdly. 'I don't want to but I must.'

'There's no must about it.' Gale spoke decidedly. The situation was melodramatic and disapproval had drowned fear decently. He said again: 'There's no must about it. I can see you're very ill indeed and we don't hang sick men in England.'

'It's not hanging I'm afraid of.'

'Then?'

Ernest didn't answer. Gale, wholly embarrassed, saw he was crying bitterly. He took another step forward.

'Stop!'

'This is utterly ridiculous. If you shoot me there are others.'

'Yes, I know.'

'Then give me the rifle.'

The weakening voice said: 'Never.'

'Then you're forcing me to take it.' Gale began to move forward quickly and the bullet caught and spun him. It was the shoulder, he guessed, but it didn't quite stop him. He fell heavily across the bed, reaching for the rifle with the arm he could still control. Ernest fought him for it feebly and swung him towards the door again. Two men had appeared in it. One had a pistol readied but the other knocked his arm up. Russell in three long strides was at the bed. He took the rifle from Ernest and handed it to Bolton.

'We heard a shot.'

'There was.' Gale was across the bed still and Russell helped him upright.

'Where did he hit you?'

'Shoulder, I think.' Gale put his other hand to it, for the first time feeling pain.

'You were lucky.'

The two men stood back. Russell held Gale and both looked at Ernest. He had slumped off his pillows, his head in his hands.

He was laughing insanely.

Chapter Seventeen

Russell and the Princess Nahid were talking to Gale in the showpiece hospital. He had a private room and was out of pain and comfortable, for as Russell had said he'd been lucky. He bore a flesh wound and one broken bone but he could fly back to England on a stretcher. A special aircraft was being sent for him, for he was still one of Her Majesty's Principal Secretaries of State. And just as well he was so, he thought cheerfully. He had work on his plate and an appetite renewed for it.

Charles Russell was recapitulating. 'So that settles Ernest.'

'You mean *you've* settled Ernest.'

'Not at all. I told you before I'm no sort of psychiatrist, but I know a nervous breakdown when I see one. That's an old-fashioned word so we'll have to prop it up a bit. In court, I mean—with so-called expert witnesses. But that won't be difficult. We'll summon the customary menagerie from the less reputable side of Wimpole Street. Then detention during Her Majesty's pleasure. I wouldn't want Ernest hanged.'

'You admire him?'

'I respect him.'

'So I had gathered.' The Foreign Secretary considered. 'Suppose your headshrinkers disagree?'

'Of course they will, they always do. We'll pick a Freudian and a pragmatist and a Pavlovian for good measure. When the dust has come down again there'll be a great deal uncertain, but in a sense it's the dust which matters. Is Ernest sane— who knows? Is he fit to be hanged? But that's very different.'

'You've a refreshing disrespect for pretentious persons.'

'I know how to use them.'

'Then I leave Ernest to you.' The Foreign Secretary spoke with a relief he wasn't hiding. 'And the politics are for me.'

It wasn't in fact a hint but Russell took it. As he rose Gale said easily: 'But there are two things you should know before you leave. First, there's no danger of invasion across the frontier. I've had a telegram from the Prime Minister, and our next-door ambassador isn't quite the same kettle as our lately lamented Resident. He's younger for one thing, and he had a few simple cards which he played with modest competence. So we shan't have our hands forced, we needn't call troops and be pilloried for imperialism. Not this time, no, and with good sense never. I hope, I intend . . .' The Foreign Secretary left it unfinished. 'And the second concerns the shaikh.' He looked at Madame and the princess nodded. 'He's gone for good. He'll sign an instrument of abdication at our convenience and he says that he's well and happy. He owns adequate funds and he's bought himself a villa. He tells us that Cordoba is the only civilized town to live in.'

'He's not the first Arab finding Spain to his liking.' Charles Russell made urbane farewells. He kissed Madame's hand and went quickly away; he went to Bolton's bungalow. He'd received an invitation and he wanted to consider it.

In an enormous room with the snow outside the stout man had been as amiable as he knew how. He was saying to the General now: 'My sincerest congratulations.'

'We were lucky.'

'Luck doesn't exist. It's an attribute of efficiency.'

'Perhaps.'

'I insist.' The stout man drummed with spatulate fingers on the leather-topped table. 'You think your friend Russell has guessed the whole story?'

'I rather doubt the whole of it. Someone tried to kill Ernest—that's better than guessing—and we're the only other people with a motive. Whether he's guessed the reason we were forced to I don't know, but I doubt if he thinks we deliberately misled him from the start. He isn't a man to stand for that and he has more than one way of conveying his disapproval. But I haven't had a word from him, only a picture postcard for my birthday. God knows how he discovered it. And unless Ernest tells him, which I'm quite sure he won't, he has no means of knowing that our oriental friends *did* play, that they did recall Ernest and that he flatly disobeyed them.' The General shook his handsome head. 'No, Russell will assume that our first plan hit a snag: either the blackmail was successfully resisted or else you yourself declined to authorize its use. My guess would be the latter.'

'Looking at it from London that'd be sound deduction. But your Colonel-friend isn't angry that you later committed trespass?'

'If he is he isn't showing it. And I don't think he'd be angry. He isn't at all a pompous man, and we still had a common interest in Ernest's removal. And in effect that's what's happened. We failed ourselves but we set it up for Russell.' The General smiled. 'He's probably laughing his head off at our Muscovite incompetence.'

'You value this new relationship?' The stout man was bland as the diplomats he despised.

'Very highly indeed.'

'Then I'll ask him on a bear shoot. . . . You think he's ever shot a bear?'

'I really don't know. You'd like me to find out?'

The stout man waved a muscular hand. 'My dear Colonel-General! A detail for the officials.'

'I'm one of them too.'

"You are when you make a rare mistake. This wasn't one of them, or not as it worked out. So we'll ask Colonel Russell here.'

'To shoot a bear?'

'A big Russian bear.' The stout man laughed immoderately at what struck him as very funny. His humour was less developed than his proven political skills.

'Mind your back if you do.'

'But why?'

'He's English, you know. You have to watch them.'

The villa wasn't extravagant for nor was Shaikh Ali, but it was comfortable, on a little hill, and the town drowsed below it in the late afternoon. Shaikh Ali was happy and his Spanish was improving. That was important since his housekeeper must understand him. He was making a proposition. All those women, he thought, those boring women; they'd almost destroyed him. But this was a good one.

Nevertheless he had hesitated, for he was a man of strict honour. It had been one thing for a reigning shaikh to summon some woman who'd never consider refusing. And money hadn't come into it. He'd never been rich but he'd had enough.

And now he was poor—three million at most. It was certain he couldn't buy her.

He put his proposal in his best and most flowery Spanish. He wasn't, he said, as young as she (this was untrue but he said it beautifully) and he was anything but Croesus; he could offer certain advantages, but they weren't very many. To a woman of her beauty, her distinction and ancient family. . . .

He went on in this vein for some time.

It went down very well indeed. The shaikh's housekeeper was a Spaniard and she would have died before talking money first, but since he had brought the subject up. . . .

She asked with the shattering candour of her race: 'How much?'

He told her apologetically.

Her face didn't change much. 'We could live on that with care.' She began to laugh musically. 'Besides,' she said, 'you've a lovely beard.'

When Russell had left them Gale talked to Madame again. He had plans for the shaikhdom and he intended to see them through. He could, he'd decided, quite easily now, for it hadn't escaped a Minister's mind that his position as a Minister had strengthened considerably. Previously he'd been dependent on the Prime Minister's sheer need of him, but now he was a hero. No, that would be vulgar—much worse, it was inept—but he knew exactly the Sunday newspaper to which he'd given an interview. It was famous for doing profiles and the facts, after all, were there. FOREIGN SECRETARY TACKLES COMMUNIST GUNMAN—good God no, not on Sundays. One must expect that in the Threepennies and it wouldn't be affectation to detest it. But when it came to an exclusive he knew precisely where to go for it. They'd underwrite it beautifully and nothing was more effective. And he must visit the House with his shoulder in a sling still, but he'd say nothing at all and he'd deprecate all compliments. One didn't become a Queen's Counsel without something of an actor's skills. His own was underplaying, he was excellent at the throwaway.

So he was talking to Madame with both enthusiasm and confidence. . . . The Council wouldn't do at all, they must re-think the whole position. They'd send an Agent who knew his job—that part could stand—and a Resident at headquarters who wasn't simply an anachronism. But it would have to go further than that. He'd offer British civil servants and he'd send the Sikhs packing. Then re-draft the Treaty, accepting proper responsibility. A positive programme of economic development. Political too as the other grew. Somehow lift the whole shaikhdom across the three centuries it had missed.

He was bubbling almost boyishly and she listened with real affection. It was cruel to disillusion him but some time she'd have to. It was kinder to strike cleanly. She said softly: 'But my dear, that won't do.'

'Why not?' He was astonished and showed it. 'I thought you wanted progress and——'

'I do. It's just that you've forgotten something.'

'What?'

'Sayyid, my cousin. He was Ali's heir and now he's shaikh.'

'But I hadn't forgotten him.' Vincent Gale was indignant. 'Indeed we've got to find him quick. If we can't find a shaikh we're faced with a different problem—worse.'

'He's found, my dear. He came to my house last night.' For a second she hesitated, then added casually: 'I think I'm going to marry him.'

'You told me he was a clerk,' Gale said. It sounded shockingly inadequate.

'He is—what's that to do with it? Naturally it's a marriage of convenience. You've said more than once that I should be shaikh and secretly I've agreed with you. But this is a Moslem country and I can't be.' She smiled at him, a cool fond smile. 'So I'm going to do a Pompadour.'

'You're crazier than Ernest.'

'I don't think I am. I know what I want here and I'll be grateful for your help in it. But I want it done our way, not yours.'

He lit the princess's cigarette, smoking most of his own in silence. At last he asked: 'And us—ourselves?'

'What's so different? I hate sounding pompous but this

is an act of policy. Sayyid's an amiable little manny and I can operate behind him. But he doesn't attract me at all. And on the other side of the medal it'll be something to know the Foreign Secretary.'

He said dryly: 'Something useful?'

'I've always found it pleasant too.'

'You're proposing another alliance, then?'

'Don't we have one already? I'll give up the London *pied-à-terre* but I'll keep on the flat in Nice. If I go there twice a year, let's say, I don't think Shaikh Sayyid will be too stupid in my absence.'

'Pompadours work hard,' he said.

'Then they also deserve their holidays. And we'll always have plenty to talk about. The frights I'm going to give you, though, my dreadful left-wing advisers! But I'll accept your civil servants. And first send me somebody who understands money. Which means not from the Treasury.'

'I still think you're crazy.'

'We'll work it out—together. We're not so far apart, I think. Not now.'

The Foreign Secretary said doubtfully: 'I suppose I can't stop you.'

'I don't see how you really can. And after all I'm offering you certain advantages. Political advantages if you care to play along with me, and others if you're still interested.'

'More than ever,' he said.

Russell seldom drank whisky before six o'clock but this evening he was making an exception. He was lying in a long cane chair in Geoffrey Bolton's bungalow and thinking that the whole affair could easily have turned out worse. Charles Russell was satisfied, for in the Security Executive that was all you could reasonably hope for bar the occasional break of quite undeserved good fortune. You played it for the minimum loss and sometimes the play came off. When it did you drank whisky early.

He looked at the ice in the very long tumbler. It particularly pleased him that Ernest was alive still. He fought his enemies with gusto but it was easy to respect them; he liked to win but he killed only when he had to. Morality didn't touch on this, it was simply that killing was clumsy. So Ernest would enter some high stone wall and there he'd await the Pleasure.

That was seemly, that was civilized.

Yes, killing was too easy. He wouldn't even kill that bear. He'd accept since he couldn't offend a friend, a valuable friend especially, but no black bear need fear him. He'd killed animals as a younger man but now he'd lost the taste for it. Instead he'd take a camera and all of them would laugh at him. Charles Russell shrugged indifferently. Let them laugh their Muscovite heads off.

He finished the whisky, walking out to the veranda. It was possible to imagine that it was two degrees cooler, and he strolled across the compound, down to the sea. The town sweltered to the left of him, beyond it the Terminal shimmered in the heat haze. It had given them some trouble, that damned town: they couldn't arrest a murderer there, or not without risking a major riot. . . . Sikhs—they were out. They were as out-of-date as liveried thugs and equally provocative. Not that Bolton would be jobless when they went. The Executive could always use Geoffrey Boltons.

And there'd have to be other changes too. Gale hadn't finished when he'd mentioned his intentions, but Russell was sure he had changed his plans. And high time too. Oil was important, but the realities of power were more so, and it was lunatic to suppose that ships down the Coast and a handful of aircraft could guarantee the flow of it. Nor all the Queen's horses and all the Queen's men—they couldn't produce a barrelful. But if the chips went down Gale would be holding one of them. Not a bad one at all though it didn't wear a uniform.

Charles Russell turned landwards. . . . A hundred miles

by twenty of screaming desert. Oil came across it and oil must be bought. It must also be sold in a buyers' market. If they saw it that way at long long last there were things which they could do still. This game of footie-footie with feudal shaikhs—an end to it. The mystiques of the oil trade and of men like the Resident—strip them ruthlessly away. But they'd left it alarmingly late.

Colonel Russell frowned thoughtfully. He wasn't a rich man but nor was he poor and he managed investments shrewdly. He turned to the molten sea again, to the arrogant ugly Terminal.

It was time to switch his oil shares.